HONESTY MP

by
Dee Aitchison

GET Publishing

Dedication

For

Peasfurlong Integrity Honesty, born 8th November 1996

and

Ingleden Integrity Honesty, born 12th November 2004

and

all the others that they represent.

~

First published in Great Britain in 2007
by Miss Delaine Haynes ridgnorth, Shropshire WV15 5DG
27 Alberbury Drive
SHREWSBURY etpublishing.co.uk
SY1 4TA

Copyright © Dee Aitchison 2007

ISBN 978-0-9556464-4-7

All the characters in this book are fictitious and any resemblance to any real person or persons, living or dead, is purely coincidental.

All rights reserved. No part of this publication may be reproduced in any form or by any means, graphic, electronic or mechanical, including photocopying, recording, taping or information storage and retrieval systems - without the prior written permission of the publisher.

Printed and bound in the United Kingdom by
Hobbs the Printers Ltd, Brunel Road, Totton, Hampshire, SO40 3WX

Honesty MP

Chapter one

Summer was past it peak, but the days were still long enough to extend into the evenings. Tom Leach and his companion walked across the yard of Coatewood Farm toward the loose boxes where cows who were due to calve, were bedded down awaiting the births. They peered in at each of the three cows. Two would not calve tonight, but the third cow moved around the box restlessly. A big white Holstein with a sprinkling of black spots, she was known by her pedigree name, Coatewood Surfer Honesty. The two men looked at her, as she shifted about in the clean deep straw. She was one of Mr Leach's favourite cows. They leaned on the half door.

'I hope it's not a bull calf,' Mr Leach said. 'It hurts when they have to go,' he admitted. 'It hurts here.' He put a large hand to his heart.

'It's all politics,' his companion replied soberly. 'We who breed and rear the animals don't have any say in it. Someone who's got no experience of rearing animals, makes a pronouncement and the next thing you know, all the papers are shouting that the animals are a risk to human health, that the meat isn't safe to eat, and ten of thousands of animals are sent for slaughter.'

Mr Leach nodded. 'My family have lived here for a hundred years and things are as bad as I've ever known, it seems everyone's got a say in how I run the farm, with rules and regulations to back them up, and all the time I'm earning less and less money. Sometimes I think I will sell up - but I know I couldn't do that - like I say, farming's been in my blood for five generations. I can't give up now.'

As he spoke Honesty strained, and a small pale coloured hoof appeared from beneath her tail.

'Three of my best cows had to go last month - slaughtered on the instructions of the Ministry,' he said. 'We have no say in the matter.'

'Nor do they,' the other man replied, nodding towards Honesty, as a small black and white body slithered onto the straw. The two men went into the shed.

'It's a heifer,' Mr Leach said with delight, as Honesty moved around and started to lick her new daughter.

'Which bull did you use,' his friend enquired as they went back outside again.

'Integrity,' Mr Leach replied.

The two men watched as Honesty nuzzled her calf.

'Honesty and Integrity,' the man mused. 'That calf should go into politics - if she did she'd be the only one in Parliament embodying either honesty or integrity,' he said, cynically. The two men turned and walked back to the farmhouse and the little calf lifted her head and blinked at the world.

~

Ten months later the spring sunshine was growing stronger with each day. The farm was becoming increasingly active as the tractors drove to and from the fields. The cows sensed that the seasons were changing and looked longingly towards the gate that led to the summer pastures. They knew that very soon one day after being milked, the gate into the winter sheds would remain closed, the field gate would be opened and they would be free to race across the fields, udders swinging as they bucked and cavorted. As their excitement subsided their noses would drop to the ground and they would commence the pleasurable feast of fresh green grass. There had been a number of new heifer calves born throughout the year and these were penned together according to their age. They would go out later in the season and graze the fields further away from the farm.

That spring several young men and women had been meeting together at regular intervals, discussing how they could further their own social lives and at the same time assist any worthy cause that could benefit from their endeavours. They were farmers' sons and daughters, and also others whose families lived in the local area.

'Has anyone got any new ideas?' A dark haired young man, aged in his early to mid twenties, who was chairman of the group, looked at his companions.

'Barn dances always go down well,' someone replied.

'Yes, but we had one last September. I was thinking perhaps we could do something different - to let people know what's been happening to our farms and villages over the past few years.'

'How do you propose to go about it,' another asked.

'Well seeing as it's election year this year, I think we should do something that would draw the voters attention to what's going on - it may even influence the politicians.'

The young man looked expectantly around the group.

'I can't see as anything we do will make very much difference,' one lad replied.

'Don't be such a defeatist, Tim', the other said. 'We need to get people's attention. Then we can show how small rural communities have suffered as the result of government policies over the past decade or so. That may lead to popular support. Politicians court popular support at election time.'

The others looked less than convinced.

'Jack's right,' a young woman with long blonde hair, seated beside Jack spoke up. 'If we are going to raise these issues at all - we need to do it now.'

'We need something people will notice, something that will get them talking,' the young man enthused. 'We need to grab their attention - something out of the ordinary.'

There was silence as they each pondered the possibilities.

'Well Jack,' one lad said quietly. 'My Dad mentioned

something a few months back that I think may be just what you are looking for.'

~

Mr Leach looked up as three young men and one young woman approached.

'Hello,' one of the young men greeted him. 'Mr Leach?'

Mr Leach nodded.

'I'm Jack Watson, my father farms over by Cawthorne Hill.' He paused. Recognition crossed Mr Leach's face. 'Yes, I know your father. What can I do for you?'

The four young people looked at each other.

'I understand you have a young heifer named Honesty, is that right?' Mr Leach nodded.

'Sired by Integrity,' Jack continued. Mr Leach nodded again.

'Well the thing is, you see,' Jack said 'We are all members of the Cawthorne Young Farmers Club and we were wondering if you could let us have her for one of our fund raising drives.'

'You'd better come in the house,' Mr Leach said. He led the way and the four young people followed him.

'Now what's this about wanting to borrow Honesty? What do you intend to do with her?'

'It's like this, sir,' one of the other young men replied. 'We heard that you had a heifer that bore the names of Honesty and Integrity.' He paused. 'And with the General Election coming up in May we thought if we took her around the towns and villages, suggesting that the voters elect her to Parliament, they may be prepared to make some donations to our funds, and at the same time we could get some publicity for the pressures which farming and rural life is under at the moment.'

Mr Leach laughed. 'I like the idea,' he said. 'Mind you I'd have to be satisfied that she was well looked after.'

'Of course,' the young man replied. The others now relaxed visibly and became animated with their ideas as they explained their plans.

'With your permission we would keep her at Jack's dad's farm. We would halter train her and treat her as if she was going to be shown. Beth here has shown calves before,' the young man looked towards the blonde haired girl. 'We would then take her out in the trailer in the evenings and at week ends, and lead her round the villages and maybe take her into town.'

Mr Leach scratched his head. 'It sounds like a good idea,' he said slowly. 'I'll need to have a word with John Watson about this before I can make a decision.'

'Yes of course,' the young people replied.

'Give me a few days,' he said, 'and I'll get back to you.'

The young people thanked him and left, and Mr Leach gazed across at the barn and wondered at Honesty's forthcoming debut.

~

Beth turned off the hose-pipe and moved the buckets and brushes out of the way. She untied Honesty's halter from the rail and led the heifer away. The young animal stepped forward confidently. The past few weeks of being led around the farm had paid off, and she now walked quietly and confidently on a halter rope.

'Hi Beth,' Jack Watson approached her. 'I've hitched the trailer up. We can take her to Witherington this afternoon.'

Honesty walked up the ramp into the trailer. She was getting used to this now. She was also getting used to the apple or similar fruit or vegetable treat she regularly received at such times, and definite character traits were beginning to become evident in certain situations. If the expected treats were not forthcoming she would sometimes stand her ground and look about, as if to indicate that part of the bargain was missing.

Jack pulled into the lay-by next to the village green. **'VOTE FOR INTEGRITY HONESTY'** stated the large black and white banner attached to the side of the trailer. Passers by stared at the trailer as Jack and two other young men opened the back and Beth led the heifer out. Positioning themselves to the front and rear of Beth and Honesty, the young people sporting black and white rosettes walked up the village street handing out leaflets, while Tim, who had drawn the short straw, walked several paces behind with a broom and shovel.

Outside the village store they stopped and Jack addressed the small group of curious shoppers who had gathered around them.

'Ladies and gentlemen,' he said. 'May I introduce our prospective parliamentary candidate, Integrity Honesty.' One or two people moved away and a small girl came forward and stroked Honesty's flank.

'We believe,' he spoke loudly, 'that this young heifer is the best candidate to represent our interests in Parliament.'

'She couldn't do any worse than them as is there already,' one man said.

'Exactly,' replied Jack. 'She is born and bred in the countryside. She will represent our rural interests – and most importantly she will live up to her name, she will act with Honesty and Integrity.' One of the young men who had accompanied them from the farm clapped enthusiastically.

'Please can we rely on your votes,' Jack shouted. 'We need your votes to elect her to Parliament.'

The people smiled, took the proffered leaflets and moved away. As one or two customers left the shop, the shopkeeper emerged.

'What's all this then?' he enquired.

Jack and the others explained their mission.

'Good luck to you,' he replied. 'We need someone like that to represent the interests of people like myself. Have you registered her as a candidate?'

'Well, no,' Jack said, somewhat surprised.

'If you do register her as a candidate I'll certainly vote for her,' the shopkeeper replied affably. 'And I'll put up your posters in my shop.'

He went into the shop and came out again a few seconds later with an apple which was readily accepted by Honesty.

'I wonder if that constitutes a donation which needs to be declared,' Beth whispered to her companions.

~

Jack looked at the papers in front of him. He had never been involved in anything like this before. On the whole, the reception they had received from people as they had toured the villages, had been positive in the extreme and many had promised their votes. Honesty's fame had gone ahead of her, particularly after a local newspaper reporter and photographer had accompanied them on one of their outings. The other members at the Young Farmers Club had become increasingly enthusiastic and at a recent meeting had voted overwhelmingly to register Honesty as an official parliamentary candidate.

Now Jack had the necessary forms to complete, with himself acting as her registered carer. Work was also increasing for other members of the team. No longer just a publicity stunt, they now found that they were spreading a message, and people were taking them seriously.

'You've done what!' Mr Watson looked at his son incredulously.

'We've decided to officially register Honesty as a parliamentary candidate,' Jack replied quietly.

'Good grief, we'll be the laughing stock of the whole country,' Mr Watson exclaimed.

'But there are issues that need to be brought to people's attention,' Jack continued. 'Honesty will be a means of doing that.'

'You can still do it without making a heifer an official candidate,' his father replied.

'But without official recognition we will regarded as no more than a YFC publicity stunt,' Jack said earnestly. 'I know from speaking to people than they want a change, they want the problems they are facing recognised, but they feel they are being patronised by all the political parties, who have neither interest nor intention in representing their concerns.'

'Have you thought this through,' his father said. 'There must surely be legalities involved.'

'I have checked up and there appear to be no rules that state that a candidate has to be a human being,' Jack replied.

'Well I hope you know what you are doing,' his father said, resignedly.

~

Throughout the course of the next few weeks, Jack, Beth and other members of the club worked hard touring around the whole of the constituency. Honesty herself became used to walking on and off the trailer. She seemed to know what was expected of her and responded tolerantly to being fussed and petted - accepting a variety of fruit and vegetables with enthusiasm.

Jack for his part was finding a new vocation as a spokesman on her behalf. Already well aware of the problems facing farmers and the rural community in general, he discussed issues effecting them, promising that if Honesty were elected he would serve them as her spokesman.

At the hustings, Jack would sit on stage with the other

candidates, while after a token appearance outside the hall, Honesty remained bedded down in the trailer.

At first the audience was mildly amused and the other candidates condescending, but as the young man answered the questions with confidence and obvious sincerity, the audience took him seriously, and the other candidates became less friendly.

'What does Honesty think of those who chase and kill in the name of sport?' he was asked.

'She considers any abuse of animals as unacceptable - and wrong - in whatever form it takes, whether by cruel farming methods, or so called traditional pursuits,' Jack replied. 'To claim that hunting live animals - with its ritualistic cruelty and displays of arrogance - is a necessary component of country life is fallacious. Such statements can adversely affect public opinion regarding the real problems faced by many farmers and the wider rural community at this time.'

'Perhaps our bovine candidate would like to express an opinion on the export of animals for slaughter,' one of the other candidates remarked, with a sly smirk at Jack.

'My understanding of Honesty's thoughts on the matter,' Jack replied, 'is that she appreciates the necessity of meat consumption by the human population, but regards the welfare of all animal species as paramount. She would support a trade in carcasses, humanely slaughtered - but she would stand against the live export of her fellow species.'

A murmur among the audience and some clapping indicated to Jack that his response had been well received, and as he left the hall later a few quiet words of appreciation and support gave him added encouragement.

~

The day of the election dawned bright and clear. Jack drove Honesty to the local polling station and tied her to the trailer. She was now very well known in the district and a photographer from the local newspaper came and took a photograph. The response from the electors continued to be good.

'Yes, I've voted for Honesty,' they said as they left the polling station. Jack smiled and thanked them, joining in the pretence that the heifer had actually garnered some votes. It had been a good few weeks. He had given interviews to a number of newspapers and a regional television crew. He had even taken one or two telephone calls from overseas. He considered he had raised awareness of the problems currently facing farming and rural communities - and that, in general, he had achieved his objectives.

That evening Jack and his friends, but without Honesty on this occasion, drove to the county town where the votes were to be counted. He felt obliged to be there as the representative of one of the candidates. As the counting got under way there seemed to be softly spoken comments passing between those sitting at the tables. Time passed and the officials moved around, as the people counting the ballot papers placed them in piles on the tables.

'It seems your cow has got some votes,' one of the officials said to Jack.

'Really?' he replied, rather taken aback, while his companions grinned at the prospect of Honesty possibly gaining more votes than some of the other independent candidates.

As the evening wore on the atmosphere in the room became increasingly charged. By this time everyone was aware that Honesty had not only gained a sizable number of votes, but that it was becoming increasingly likely that she was going to have a majority. Groups of people huddled in corners, whispering to each other with looks of concern on their faces. Officials hurried in and out of the room. Newspaper reporters were now gathering outside and Jack was beginning to feel besieged.

Chapter two

The returning officer took Jack aside. He looked pale.

'I have ordered a recount,' he said, 'but I think there is no longer any doubt history has been made tonight.' He paused, 'But I cannot see that your cow will be able to take her seat in Parliament.'

Once Jack had realised what had happened, he was at first unsure whether or not to accept Honesty's election. His friends were divided on what he should do. Some said 'Go for it, Jack, take her to Westminster.' Others advised caution and suggested he should say that, with regret, he could not accept her election and leave the electorate free to vote again. But as he thought about all the people he had met over the past few weeks, how they had expressed their concerns to him, how they had told him what they were experiencing, Jack knew he could not let them down. They had voted for Honesty because they no longer believed that politicians of any party were to be trusted. They had believed that Jack was sincere when he had told them that he would make sure Honesty allowed their voices to be heard. He would honour that and was prepared to carry through Honesty's representation of the people.

'I appreciate your concern, sir,' he replied politely, 'but I fully intend to allow Honesty to take up the position she has been elected to. I will assist her in every way I can.'

The returning officer did not reply. In all his years of officiating at election counts, nothing had prepared him for what had happened tonight. He was fully conversant with all the procedures involved, but there was nothing to advise him how to proceed when an animal had been elected.

'Of course you will have to bring her in when the results of the recount are announced,' he said, in the hope of gaining more time.

'She's at home,' Jack replied. 'I will go and fetch her.'

Jack spoke with his friends and they hurried out the door, fortunately unrecognised by the newsmen and women now thronging outside. As they left, the first of the television crews were arriving.

Lights were on at the farm when they got home. Jack went to the kitchen door as his friends went to attach the trailer to the Land Rover.

'Jack, whatever's going on.' Mrs Watson appeared in the kitchen in her dressing gown. 'We've been receiving all manner of phone calls. It is impossible to get any sleep. Your father is furious.'

Before Jack could answer, Mr Watson came through the door.

'I've just about had enough of this nonsense,' he said angrily. 'First you put a heifer up as a parliamentary candidate, now I'm woken up in the small hours by goodness knows who telling me she's been elected as an MP.'

'It's true, Dad,' Jack replied quietly. His parents stared at him.

'Say that again,' his father said slowly.

'It's true. She's been elected. I have been at the Town Hall all evening. She got a majority of the votes. We have come to fetch her. She needs to be there when the announcement is made.'

Mr Watson sat down. He didn't speak. The phone rang again and Mrs Watson went to answer it.

'And I'm going to accept on her behalf.' Jack said as he went through the door.

His father stared after him, too stunned to reply.

Jack's friends went into the little paddock where Honesty had spent the early summer when she had not been on tour. Only a light sleeper she was not unusually perturbed by the young people as they approached her.

Outside the Town Hall crowds were gathered round the front entrance.

'I think we might do better to go round the back.' one of the young men said. But too late, the Land Rover and trailer had already been spotted and newsmen surged around. Jack slowly manoeuvred the vehicle towards the door.

The ramp was lowered and Beth went inside the trailer with the halter.

'Come on, sweetheart,' she said softly in Honesty's ear. 'Come and meet your constituents.'

As they emerged from the trailer, a cheer went up and flash lights exploded all round. Honesty gazed around her in amazement. A ramp leading into the building, designed for wheelchair access, was ideal for the young heifer to enter the Town Hall.

Once inside she remained near the door, while Jack joined the other candidates on the stage.

The returning officer announced the results.

'And I hereby declare Coatewood Integrity Honesty the elected member for this constituency.'

There were cheers and clapping. 'HON-EST-Y! HON-EST-Y! HON-EST-Y!' the crowds called her name as she twisted her ears in their direction.

Jack took the microphone and gave a short acceptance speech on her behalf.

'You may rest assured I will faithfully interpret her instructions,' he said. 'And I look forward to serving you all in my capacity as her spokesman and interpreter.'

Honesty and Jack took a photo call as they stood on the steps of the Town Hall. His friends formed a phalanx around her as they made slow progress towards the trailer.

'Jack! Jack!' the throng of reporters and cameramen pressed around him, bombarding him with questions. Jack spoke with the reporters, assuring them that, yes indeed, he fully intended that she would represent her constituents. She had been elected to do a job, and he would ensure that it was carried out to the best of both their abilities.

~

The sky on the eastern horizon was starting to lighten as the Land Rover and trailer pulled into the farmyard. At least the newsmen and women had not arrived there yet. From the milking parlour came a steady pulse of the milking machines as his father milked the cows. Honesty was returned to her paddock, and Jack sank down in the chair beside the kitchen range. The adrenalin that had kept him going for the past few hours had subsided and he now he felt as if his arms and legs were made of lead.

'You'd best get an hour or twos sleep,' his mother said as she handed him a drink. 'I think we are going to have a very busy day today.'

'Thanks, Mum,' he said. 'I hope Honesty and I are going to be up to it.'

'Of course you will. Just don't forget what her names stand for - that's why people voted for her and that's what they'll expect of you.'

Jack stood up and headed towards the stairs.

~

Three hours later Jack was awake again. He looked out of the window. Now there was a large number of vehicles parked along the farm drive, some with satellite dishes on the roof. In the lane he could see police officers placing "No Waiting" cones. His mother was right - it was going to be a busy day.

Downstairs, the kitchen was empty. Jack switched on the small television set standing on the worktop. The first picture that appeared on the screen was of himself and Honesty standing outside the Town Hall the previous night.

The camera then moved to a reporter interviewing some of the people.

'Did you vote for Honesty?' she enquired of one lady.

'Yes I did,' the woman replied.

'Why was that?'

'Because I no longer believe that the party candidates can be trusted to represent us. They are dishonest with us - that's why I voted for Honesty.'

'But she is an animal,' the reporter persisted. 'She cannot speak on your behalf in Parliament.'

'She might be an animal, but at least she is independent - and she is not going to be influenced by party political or other interests, like those other MPs.'

The reporter turned to another voter and Jack recognised the shopkeeper who had been one of the first people to support Honesty as an official candidate.

'Why did you vote for Honesty?' the reporter enquired.

'Honesty - and Jack Watson - are local. They know what has been happening to our villages and the wider rural community over the past few years,' the man said. 'The political decision makers are too close to vested interests. For years we've needed honesty and integrity in Westminster - now we've got them.'

The reporter turned to the camera. 'There is a lot of anger with the old political order here,' she said. 'People are telling me that before Honesty stood as a candidate there was little point in voting - they did not feel that their concerns would be heard. It now seems that a cow has given them a voice.'

Jack turned off the television as Mr Watson came in through the door, throwing his cap on a chair.

'I'm supposed to be running a farm, not a circus,' he

cried in exasperation. 'I,ve spent half the morning directing news reporters and their vehicles - the driver of the milk tanker wasn't able to get into the yard. They all want to speak to you.' Mr Watson sat down. 'I had to tell them you would be out later.'

'Yes, they will expect a press conference.' Jack agreed. 'I will arrange it for 11 o'clock, if that's OK with you.' He looked towards his father.

'Suits me,' he replied. 'So long as I can have my farm back when you've finished.'

'I'll tell them that's the deal,' Jack said.

The newsmen and women had positioned themselves in the farmyard where they had come to an agreement with Mr Watson on what they required and what he could accommodate.

At 11 o'clock Jack collected Honesty from the paddock, and together they stood in front of the assembled company of pressmen and women and television cameras. This morning the questions were more considered as each of the reporters questioned Jack.

'Do you intend to stay the full term of this parliament?' they enquired. 'How do you plan to accommodate Honesty at Westminster?' 'Will you discuss proposed legislation with her?' 'How do you know what she is thinking?' 'How will you enable her to vote?'

Jack answered confidently.

Yes, he intended that she should complete the full parliamentary term. He will be having discussions as to the accommodation she will be requiring. Yes, he will talk to her about any subject which will require her participation as an MP, but the interpretation of her wishes would be his alone.

As they were both born and brought up on farms in this constituency, Jack stated that he was confident that he could faithfully translate her wishes. He explained that when this question had arisen during canvassing prior to the election, the voters had been satisfied with what he had proposed and cast their votes accordingly. When Honesty was required to vote in Parliament he would be guided by whatever procedures were put in place.

Following the questions, the cameramen followed Jack and Honesty back to the paddock, where they posed by the field gate, and the photographs subsequently appeared in newspapers and magazines around the world.

The media gleefully reported on the fact that the only previous animal to have an official position in government had been when the Roman Emperor Caligula had appointed his horse as a Senator - where the horse enjoyed the reputation as the wisest and least harmful of them all. But in this case Honesty had been elected by the will of the people, although the similarities between the Roman Senators the Westminster MPs remained.

~

As the newsmen and women left and the farm returned to it's normal routine, Jack was able to start thinking about how this unexpected turn of events was going to be handled. He was going to need lots of advice – not only in accommodating Honesty's position as MP, but also to gain some knowledge of what his own role would involve.

Throughout the afternoon, he took phone calls from friends and well-wishers until, early in the evening, he received the call he needed.

'Hello Jack,' a man's voice greeted him. 'My name is James Drury. I was an MP for several years. I have followed your campaign with interest, and offer my congratulations on Honesty's election.'

'Thank you,' Jack replied.

'If I can be of any help,' the caller continued, 'please don't hesitate to contact me.'

'Thank you,' Jack said again. 'What party did you belong to?'

Mr Drury gave the name of his party. 'But I didn't agree with their stance on some important issues, and fell foul of the party system. As an Independent, Honesty will be free of the constraints of the party whips – she will enable you to speak your mind and more faithfully represent your constituents' interests. I envy you,' he added.

Mr Drury then advised Jack on who he should get in touch with regarding the parliamentary timetable and what measures needed to be implemented in order for Honesty to take her place in the Commons Chamber.

Over the next few days numerous calls were made to London and Jack, accompanied by Beth, whom it was intended would act as his secretary, visited the House of Commons and made arrangements for Honesty's accommodation.

After several meetings with officials, most of whom had never had any dealings with farm animals, it was decided that a pen should be built at the far end of the Chamber, and workmen were instructed to carry out the work forthwith. A regular supply of straw bedding was ordered. As an MP, Honesty was also entitled to use the Members restaurant, tea rooms and bars, but it was eventually agreed that a hay rack and water trough in her pen would better serve both her, and the other members, interests.

The matter of her toilet requirements were also of considerable concern to the officials. It was something which Jack and his friends had encountered during the weeks of canvassing. Usually one of the group was delegated to be supplied with a shovel, a plastic bag and a supply of sawdust. This had served the situation well enough while she was paraded around the streets of the towns and villages, but now that she would be walking through the venerable halls and corridors of the Mother of Parliaments, the officials were concerned that her lack of rudimentary toilet training would be a cause of embarrassment and health concerns to everyone else.

'Can't you get her to use a specified spot,' one official asked.

'A cow wouldn't use a designated area,' Jack replied.

'We will clean up after her,' he assured them. The officials did not look reassured.

Although it was essential that Honesty should attend the Commons Chamber, especially on the occasion of important debates and subsequent voting, the matter of her accommodation outside the House was of particular importance. Initially Jack had considered renting a barn and paddock at a farm in the Home Counties, but after some discussion with Beth and his friends and advisors, it was decided that she would best be accommodated at a city farm on the outskirts of the capital. This had benefits for all concerned - it was within relatively easy reach of Westminster, any constituents wishing to visit her could get there by bus or train - and local schools, who already visited the city farm on educational visits, could learn about constitutional history at the same time.

The city farm manager was only too happy to provide her with the necessary facilities - supposing, rightly, that her presence would boost the number of visitors.

~

Jack returned home to prepare for Honesty's parliamentary debut. She herself remained quite unconcerned about it all, unaware of the furore that her election had caused. She grazed contentedly, now that the number of visitors to the farm had diminished. Jack had contacted Mr Leach to ask to buy Honesty, but the older man had not been inclined to sell.

Although the Watsons had high welfare standards on their farm, Jack had never felt particularly sentimental about most of the animals he had grown up with - but over the past few months he found himself growing increasingly close to Honesty. Now that she was no longer simply a farm animal but a representative, not only of the constituents but also of her species, he felt an obligation to really try and present things from a farm animal's point of view.

'Come on, young lady,' he would say as he scratched the poll on the top of her head. 'What do you think of this?' while he talked about the Government's agricultural policy.

As well as farming, Jack realised he would also be representing her on social issues, the environment and anything of concern to her constituents. For her part, Honesty remained silent. Her species were sometimes regarded as stupid, but their placid demeanour hid a natural curiosity - and often a sense of fun. Her face was far from expressionless and she could not only indicate pleasure and appreciation but also, on occasions, imply that she was smiling.

Jack needed to consider the maiden speech, which he would deliver on her behalf. There was so much of concern to farming and rural communities that it was difficult for him to choose a topic. But as he stood by the gate to her paddock watching her, he recognised that her election could have profound repercussions for the way in which farm animals were treated. This momentum should be built on, not only for the animal species but also to relate these potential improvements to the rest of the population. Jack recalled the Mahatma Ghandi's remark that the greatness of a nation and its moral progress can be judged by the way its animals are treated. As he watched her she raised her head, looked straight at him and silently confirmed her approval.

Chapter three

Beth and Jack collected Honesty from the field and loaded her in the trailer. She was about to take her seat, or more specifically her straw bedded pen, in Westminster. They had both packed their suitcases and were preparing to take up their positions as Honesty's staff in London. A few friends from the village and a photographer from the local newspaper came to see them off.

They settled Honesty into her new home at the city farm. She had her own separate quarters as befitted a Member of Parliament. She walked into the loose box prepared for her, where a few cards from well wishers had been pinned on the door. She explored the box, nibbled some of the fresh straw and indicated that the arrangements met with her approval. The loose box also gave access to her own small paddock, where she was able to enjoy fresh grass with the sun on her back. Satisfied that she was well cared for, Jack and Beth drove into the capital and, having dropped off their luggage, made their way to the Houses of Parliament to settle themselves into the office accommodation provided. They were shown to their office.
'You've already got some mail,' the assistant said, indicating Jack's desk. It was piled with letters and papers.
'It looks like you are going to be pretty busy,' he said to Beth, as she glanced at the envelopes, which had come from all over the world.

Over the next few days Beth got down to work.
'Because Honesty has become so well known all sorts of people are writing to us. Her diary is starting to fill up already,' she said.

Parliamentary etiquette meant that Jack was unable to respond to the problems that the constituents of many other MPs wrote to him about. But he replied to them as Honesty's representative, and noted the many similar concerns felt by farmers and rural communities throughout the country.

Meanwhile he began to make himself familiar with everything he needed to know. He was surprised at how small the Commons Chamber was. Originally built for fewer MPs than now, it certainly had not been anticipated that a pen would be required for a heifer elected as a representative of the people. An official explained that as Jack himself had not been elected, he would not be allowed to take a seat on the green leather benches. A suitable chair was found for him and placed next to Honesty's pen.

He noted when Honesty was needed to attend parliamentary sessions, and checked those which it would be possible for him to attend alone. Forthcoming debates were listed and Jack made sure that he and Honesty could attend all those that affected his constituency and those that affected farming, the environment and rural communities in general. He read as much as he could to familiarise himself on all points that might be raised.

As Beth had said, Honesty's fame had drawn an increasingly large postbag and there were many requests for her presence to attend shows, fetes and any event where her celebrity status would endorse a cause.

'I've got requests from two supermarkets for Honesty to open their new premises,' Beth remarked to Jack one morning.

'No chance,' he said angrily. 'Not while they fail to pay producers a fair price for their products. People voted for Honesty because of the disparity in what food costs to produce, and what is paid by the supermarket buyers. That's one of the things we need to highlight. Honesty comes from a long line of milk producers, her family have borne calves and produced milk for generations. It's not right that their lives and the work of the farmers is no longer given fair reward.'

'OK, I'll explain that as tactfully as I can in my reply,' Beth said. 'I've also had a request for her to open a farm shop in the Midlands.'

'Yes, we'll do that,' Jack replied immediately. 'Find out all you can and we'll go along and support their enterprise. The supermarkets have put so many small shops out of business, ventures like this should be supported. They are keeping the money within the community as well as giving the farmers a fair return for their labour and investment.'

Later that evening Jack spoke with Mr Drury again on the phone.

'How are you finding things?' the older man enquired.

'Hard work,' Jack replied. 'As well as everything being so new to me, I'm having to read so much and find out about so many related subjects.'

'I know,' the older man said, 'but don't forget that the researchers are there to help you with these things. They are very good at their jobs. You and Beth will need to use their services if you are to keep on top of all the things you will be expected to debate on.'

'Yes, we've already set one researcher to work, and Beth's doing a great job sorting out all the correspondence,' Jack said. 'Honesty's got the easiest part. All she has to do is chew her cud and look pretty, while I'm up half the night checking out all I need to know before the next day's debate.'

Mr Drury laughed. 'There are quite a few animals, and quite a few people for that matter, who would like her job. Are things shaping up as you had expected?'

'Yes,' Jack replied enthusiastically. 'I think we have the opportunity to really make a difference. Honesty's popularity with most people means that they take our message on board about the need for the truth in regard to all aspects food production and the environment. We are reaching people we couldn't have done without her – and popular support will bring about improvements for everyone concerned.'

There was a pause before Mr Drury spoke.

'I don't want to dampen your enthusiasm,' he said, 'but some things are more difficult to change than you might imagine.'

'How do you mean?' Jack enquired.

'For some time now many of the laws by which we are governed are no longer made by our MPs in Westminster.'

'Who by then?' Jack asked.

'It goes back many years,' the older man said, 'but much of our ability to govern ourselves has been signed away. It had been made out to be in everyone's best interests, but time has proved otherwise. It is for that reason that I think you will find it difficult to change some things.'

'But surely if people realised this they would protest against it.' Jack said.

'Perhaps they would,' Mr Drury replied, 'but it is generally not reported in the mass media. What is not actually suppressed, is subjected to so much misinformation that the reality is not recognised.' Jack was silent.

'I'm sorry Jack, but there are too many other influences on the way Westminster, and for that matter other governments act, for you to be able to change things as you would like. Except for Honesty, MPs are human, and fallible human beings at that. Politics attracts some people with questionable motives. The party system puts others under pressure. You have to remember that these people will serve three masters – their party, themselves and their constituents - usually in that order.'

'But there must be members who genuinely want to serve the best interests of the people they represent?' Jack said.

'Of course,' Mr Drury replied. 'Many men and women

enter politics with good intentions, but people with high ideals fall at the first fence of the selection process. A few manage to get elected, but they are soon made to conform by the whips. Also,' he continued, 'there are temptations within the corridors of power, and many have succumbed. As a heifer, Honesty cannot be compromised by favours, sexual or otherwise. By virtue of being an animal she is able to live up to her name.'

'But surely the whole point of Parliament is to act in the best interests of the electorate.' Jack insisted.

'People trust that their elected representatives will not succumb to inducements.' Mr Drury replied. 'But modern politicians and the unelected officials in government agencies and departments see themselves as Caesar's wife - beyond reproach - even if others don't see them that way. To admit that they are wrong - that a pronouncement they made or a policy they created or encouraged was fundamentally flawed - is unthinkable. Therefore the facts have to be, shall we say, "adjusted" to save face and protect reputations, careers and pensions. They are remarkably adept at it - having had plenty of practice in recent years. I know I sound cynical, but I spent several years in the House. In the end I had to take the decision to leave rather than be regarded as part of what is seen as normal in that environment.'

'The voters elected Honesty to change all that. The two of us intend to try to do what she was elected for.' Jack said stubbornly.

Mr Drury sighed. 'Your sincerity as Honesty's spokesperson is commendable, but you will be working within a system that to a large extent seeks its own preservation at whatever the cost to the country.'

~

In the maiden speech which Jack made in Parliament on Honesty's behalf he quoted the Mahatma Ghandi, and continued, 'The voters of Leythorpe Valley have taken the first step. Honesty and her kind are so often regarded as having no other value than as production units or objects of trade, even by some animal health care professionals. This attitude ignores sentience, disparages empathy, and associates emotional attachment with weakness. That mentality diminishes Society. Honesty's election has sent a signal to the world, that this nation has the capability to not only advance animal welfare but to raise standards and promote ethical behaviour in all things.'

Some MPs looked at Jack with interest, but many barely registered what he had said.

Chapter four

Honesty had been living at the city farm for a few weeks, and had made several personal appearances in the Commons Chamber. The systems put in place for her appearances had been working well and the other members, officials and parliamentary staff had got used to her presence. Jack was still getting to know both people and procedures. It seemed to him that some people deliberately ignored both Honesty and himself, but others appeared pleased to make his acquaintance, especially those members from rural constituencies, some of whom shared similar values to Jack.

~

One late afternoon some weeks after her arrival when Honesty had made one of her personal appearances in the Commons Chamber, Jack and Beth were leading her along the wide corridor with it's high decorated ceiling. Suddenly one of the researchers came over to them.

'Mr Watson, I'm so glad I've caught you. I'm working for Stephen Amies. He is the Member for one of the northern constituencies. I'm researching matters of agricultural reform for him,' he said holding out his hand. 'He has said that he would particularly like to meet you. Would it be convenient for you to see him now?'

'Well we were just going to take Honesty back to the trailer and return her to the farm,' Jack replied, 'perhaps I could meet him tomorrow.'

'I'm sorry but he will be leaving very shortly himself to visit his constituency – I know he would like to speak to you before he leaves. If you and the young lady,' he looked at Beth, 'could come now it would be very much appreciated.'

Jack looked at Beth. 'I'd like to help if I could, but we have Honesty with us and she wouldn't be able to go up the stairs.'

The man looked at Honesty, then looked about him.

'Couldn't you tie her up somewhere here, just until you have spoken to Mr Amies? There is a bar here you could tie her to.'

Beth and Jack looked where he indicated. It seemed a suitable place to leave her for a few minutes. There were very few people about and she would not be in the way. Jack tied the halter rope to the bar and Beth deposited the large holdall, containing a bucket, shovel and copious supply of sawdust, that was always carried when they escorted Honesty through the buildings.

'Mr Amies has been anxious to speak to you for a while, but so much of his time is taken up with travelling to and from his constituency, it gives him less time to get to meet people here,' the researcher said. 'It's so much easier for people representing the South East,' he added. He led them through the corridors and up the stairs and knocked on the door of the office shared by Mr Amies and two other MPs.

'Jack, I'm so pleased to see you, and you too young lady,' he said, shaking their hands. 'Do take a seat.'

'Thank you, but we've left Honesty tied up downstairs,' Jack said. 'I really oughtn't to leave her too long.'

'I won't keep you long', Stephen Amies replied, but I would like to know what you, and of course Honesty, think about this proposal.'

~

Back downstairs Honesty fidgeted. She had not been in a particularly good humour today. Jack and Beth were used to her occasional moodiness. Sometimes she was placid and contented, other times she acted as if everything was new to her and to be regarded with suspicion, and on other occasions it seemed as if she deliberately set out to be contrary. One or two people had come over to her where she was tied, but she didn't make a welcoming response and they left her alone. She shifted her feet. She didn't like it here. She was bored, there was no hay or straw to nibble. She wanted to lie down, but Jack had kept the halter rope short and she had to remain standing.

Two women approached her. 'Hello there, you must be Honesty,' one woman said with a slight American accent. She went up to her and stroked the side of her neck. Honesty ignored her.

'You are very pretty,' the woman said, looking into her face. She turned to her companion, 'Hasn't she got the most beautiful eyes.' Honesty scowled. 'What's the matter, honey?' she said as Honesty shifted about. 'Oh, this rope you are tied with is so short, you can't move about properly.' The woman untied the rope.

'Should you be doing that?' her companion said eyeing Honesty warily.

'I'm only giving her a bit more rope,' the woman said amiably, as she wrapped the halter rope round the bar.

'There, you can move about better now, can't you,' she said giving Honesty another stroke on her back. 'The British really do take their love for animals to extremes,' she said as they walked away.

Honesty watched them go. Extra rope was all well and good but she really would prefer her straw bed. She stepped backwards, pulling on the rope. As she lifted her head the rope unravelled from the bar and fell to the floor. Honesty took another couple of steps and discovered that she could now move about without restraint. She looked about her and decided that an investigation of her surroundings might lead to the discovery of some hay or straw. With the rope dangling from her halter she sniffed about. On one side of the hallway a carpeted corridor led off into another part of the building. Honesty proceeded to extend her search.

~

'I very much admire what you are doing for rural communities,' Mr Amies said to Jack and Beth. 'You've raised the profile of what is happening far better than any amount of speeches by people such as myself.'

'It's not me, it's Honesty,' Jack replied, seated comfortably in his chair. 'Without her very few people would have listened to me. I just wanted to raise those issues during the run up to the election. I never expected her to be elected.'

'I'm afraid I will have to leave now as I have a train to catch,' Stephen Amies said, standing up and lifting a brief case onto his desk. 'It's been a pleasure meeting you. I'll be in touch again when I return.'

'I look forward to meeting you again,' Jack replied, 'there's a lot we have to discuss.'

~

Two floors below, Honesty proceeded down the corridor. Where there was a choice of direction she selected a route, but further along she came to a pair of double doors that obstructed her path and she turned around. On her left a door was open. She looked inside. The small reception room was comfortably furnished with various easy chairs, dining chairs and occasional furniture. In the middle of the room was circular table, on which a floral arrangement was the centre piece. Against the one wall was a sideboard, decorated with porcelain vases and on which a coffee pot and cups and saucers had been placed. Honesty stepped inside the room. She had given up the idea of finding the desired hay and straw, but the new surroundings invited her curiosity and she investigated the room and it's contents. It was not long before her nose detected the floral decoration in the centre of the table. She leaned across and her tongue tentatively investigated the foliage. Apparently to her liking, she curled her tongue around a delicate bloom and yanked it from the vase.

~

Jack and Beth walked down the stairs, but as they entered the large hallway where they had left Honesty, there was no sign of her.

'Whatever has happened to Honesty?' Jack exclaimed. 'Surely no one has taken her away.' They both looked around them.

'Oh oh,' Beth said, 'I think I know which way she has gone,' indicating with her eyes a large cow pat at the entrance to the carpeted corridor.

'Oh, no,' Jack said and they both hurried off in pursuit. As they came to a choice of direction they looked at the floor, but there were no marks on the carpet to indicate which way Honesty had gone.

'Aargh!' A woman's scream came from the corridor to their left.

'I think we've found Honesty, or at least someone has,' Jack said as they both broke into a run.

Jack and Beth raced through the doorway, where an immaculately dressed woman was shouting at Honesty, who stood transfixed in mid chew, with an exotic crimson blossom protruding from the side of her mouth.

'I'm most terrible sorry,' Jack said, 'I don't know how she got away.'

'Whatever is going on,' two men alerted by the noise now came into the room.

'I came in here to prepare for the Ambassador's visit and found that, that...' the woman pointed at Honesty.

'Heifer?' Jack said, trying to be helpful.

'That creature in here,' the woman screamed.

By now more people had come to investigate the cause of the commotion.

Honesty, whose mood had not been too amiable before, was becoming increasingly irritated by the noise the woman was making. As the small room filled with even more people, she started to become agitated. Jack tried to get past to take hold of the halter rope, but one of the other men pushed forward shouting, 'It's OK, I'll get her.'

As the people pressed around her, Honesty pushed against the furniture and two of the dining chairs toppled over. The man trying to reach her lost his balance as he encountered the prostrate chairs and the table wobbled ominously. The woman screamed again and Honesty, who was now rapidly loosing her cool, pushed her way between the easy chairs and up against the sideboard. Another of the men hurriedly grabbed one of the porcelain vases, clutching it to his chest, and stood with his back pressed against the wall as she lumbered past.

As the confusion increased, Jack scrambled over the dining chairs, following behind Honesty - while Beth quietly approached from the other side.

'The Ambassador will be here any moment,' the woman cried hysterically. Honesty looked around agitatedly and Beth calmly took hold of the dangling rope and spoke quietly and reassuringly to her, at the same time leading her from the room.

Out in the corridor Beth and Jack led Honesty back the way they had come. Somewhat relieved that the damage hadn't been greater, they glanced at each other and then started to giggle nervously. Beth bit her lip, 'Thank goodness Honesty wasn't born a bull.'

~

A few days later Jack was surprised to receive a message that both he and Honesty were invited to attend an informal meeting. With little more information about what the meeting was about, Jack and Beth collected Honesty and took her along to the specified location at the appointed time. A wide doorway gave access to the room and a tall, distinguished man stepped forward, approaching the trio as they stood in the entrance.

'I am most honoured to meet you,' he said. 'May I

introduce myself - my name is Julio Mendez. I am from South America.'

'I'm pleased to meet you,' said Jack, already beginning to suspect that this invitation may have some connection with Honesty's embarrassing entry into another reception room a few days before.

'And so this is Honesty,' His Excellency continued. 'It is a great honour to meet such a well-known bovine personage. I understand that I nearly had the pleasure of meeting her on a previous occasion.' The other people present looked expectantly at Jack.

'Yes, I'm most terrible sorry about what happened,' Jack said.

The Ambassador smiled. 'When I heard what had occurred, I specifically requested to meet you both. I had heard of Honesty before, of course, and that she should wish to join my reception of her own free will, indicated a remarkable initiative. I am only too pleased that her unplanned appearance a few days ago has enabled me to make her acquaintance now.'

He walked towards the table. 'Would you care for a drink? I understand that the former floral arrangement was found to be to Honesty's taste.'

Jack winced. The Ambassador laughed.

'I did not think a floral arrangement would be suitable refreshment for her this morning, so I arranged for a bowl of fruit to be provided.'

The Ambassador went to a fruit bowl, and slicing an apple offered it to Honesty, who received it with relish. Her previous bad humour had passed and she looked on the present company with amiable tolerance. The embarrassment of her previous behaviour was put aside in the face of the His Excellency's good humour and thoughtfulness.

The Ambassador sat down, indicating Jack should take another chair.

'Tell me Mr Watson, how do you see Honesty's election

affecting farming in your country?'

Jack explained how he hoped that he could bring to people's notice how food, farming, animal welfare and the environment were closely connected, and by creating that attention achieve benefits for all concerned.

'Very worthy intentions,' the Ambassador remarked. 'In my country we rear large numbers of cattle. Ranching is of great importance to our economy.'

'As Honesty's spokesman,' Jack replied, 'I advocate sustainable farming, with neither detrimental effects on the livelihoods of the local people, nor on the earth and it's resources. Surely such large operations must adversely affect all of these things.'

'Your support for those issues is most worthy,' the Ambassador replied. 'And I respect your personal sincerity. However your Government's response to animal disease control in the past, and possibly in the future, has hardly been compatible with good management of either livestock, farming, the environment or your rural economy.'

Jack knew what the Ambassador was referring to and remembered the heartbreak involved and he remained silent. He thought of the anguish and grief of the farming families who lost priceless stock, and the individuals who fought desperately to save their much loved pets, the despair of the men and women whose animals, although not slaughtered, could not be moved, while the newborn suffered in appalling conditions, and their dams cried their distress. Whole communities were effected as their income dwindled, supporting each other by telephone, while men and women contracted to apply the genocide, drove vans and wagons around lanes which twelve months previously had been vibrant with life. The newborn and the pregnant mothers were not spared. It was noted that as the animals died the birds ceased to sing and a pall of desolation hung over the land. The emotional effects on the families continued for years, sometimes developing into physical illnesses.

'In my country we vaccinate the animals at the first suspicion of disease with a minimum of slaughter,' the Ambassador continued.

'Yes, so I have heard,' Jack replied. 'However, here the decisions are made by those, who are not necessarily the best qualified. Sadly too many people do not question the judgments of those given authority, be they political or scientific.' He paused. 'Honesty and I would like to raise the awareness of the need for the full facts and all options discussed openly before any decisions are made.'

'Indeed.' The Ambassador smiled kindly. 'I wish you well in your endeavours. Animal, human and economic health are all related. Interference in such matters should not be made without due consideration of all the factors involved.'

'Your country has much rainforest,' Jack continued, 'I understand that logging and monoculture crops are destroying great swathes of it every day. It's value to the rest of the world is immeasurable in terms of climate and undiscovered health remedies. Does your Government intend to take action to preserve what remains?'

'I personally agree that the preservation of the rainforest would be good for my country as well as the world - and we must always consider future generations,' the Ambassador replied. 'Many non-governmental organisations are working in my country at present, assisting the indigenous people and securing the forest, but you must understand that other powerful organisations also have designs on the land. Ruthless foreign interests apply pressure - you have a saying in your country "the carrot and the stick" - and sadly, decisions are taken that have detrimental consequences for many years to come. The world is not a just place, Mr Watson – otherwise we would all be living in Paradise.'

'Honesty was elected in response to perceived improbity,' Jack said. 'As her representative, I want to expose the origins of the pressures you refer to.'

'Ah, the idealism of youth,' the Ambassador said.

'However, Honesty has provided the means to enable you to progress. Although I suspect that many animals have her qualities, no others have as yet achieved her status.'

The Ambassador stood up. 'It has been a great pleasure to meet you, but I think perhaps Honesty should return to her stall now. It is not fair to expect her to stand here while we discuss the failings of governments.' The Ambassador went to the fruit bowl again and handed Jack and Beth some apples, pears and bananas.

'A gift from the animals of my country to the animals of yours,' he said.

Chapter five

Jack had hardly become accustomed to Westminster and parliamentary procedure before the summer recess interrupted proceedings. He was glad of the opportunity to learn more about what was expected of him as Honesty's interpreter, and he was in regular contact with Mr Drury, who provided invaluable practical advice. Beth continued to deal with the correspondence, which made little or no allowance for the parliamentary vacation.

Throughout the summer months Jack received and accepted many invitations. As far as possible he took Honesty with him. But a seemingly endless series of diseases - with no apparent political will to utilize a treatment or research a cure for the benefit of all species, animal and human - was an ongoing threat. Jack was acutely aware that if Honesty failed any of her veterinary tests, her status as an elected Member of Parliament would not save her from slaughter. Isolation and even application of an effective treatment would not be acceptable. Individual circumstances were not taken into consideration - no one was exempt. A blanket rule was applied, sometimes ruthlessly. Jack was in constant contact with the Ministry concerned - pressing, on Honesty's behalf, to use the latest scientific and technical innovations from around the world. His contact with members of the scientific community alerted him to much research which, for reasons he could only surmise, was ignored by the regulatory authorities.

He was invited to many of the agricultural shows that summer, where Honesty made guest appearances. They usually did at least one circuit of the show ring during each day. It was during these visits that Jack was able to speak with many of the people who, like Honesty's constituents, had felt sidelined by the other political parties.

'My family are stewards of our dairy herd,' he said. 'We care for them, and in their turn provide us with milk and meat. It is a symbiotic relationship. They did not choose this life. We take the decisions of life and death over them and in doing so, we have an obligation to care for them to the best of our ability. However, despite our best efforts, increasing regulation has hampered our ability to carry out our stewardship with care and compassion. Impersonal decisions by government and it's agencies - taken by people who are remote, and in some cases arrogant - and zealously implemented by the ignorant, can have devastating effects both on people and animals.'

He had received much correspondence from farmers and smallholders all over the country. Some felt at their wits' end with regulations – which bore no logic and certainly no concern for animal welfare. He understood and noted their concerns, assuring them that he would raise matters with the appropriate Minister, although he was already feeling that as an individual and independent MP, Honesty was not going the make the difference that both he and her electors had hoped.

'We need a Party that responds with comprehension and compassion, instead of relying on insensitive control,' he replied grimly to one distressed countryman.

~

Jack also visited a cottage hospital within Honesty's constituency, which was threatened with closure. It was one of the special concerns that had influenced him to campaign with Honesty before the election.

'I feel very strongly about retaining this little hospital,' he said to the duty doctor on his visit. 'People need these small community hospitals. For minor operations and convalescence they serve the community far better than the larger establishments which are usually some considerable distance away.'

The senior sister agreed. 'We find people respond

better to treatment when they are in familiar surroundings, when their relatives and friends are only a few minutes drive away. The big hospitals cannot help but be impersonal when they operate on such a large scale. Here both patients and staff are local to the area and it helps create the sort of environment in which the patients can recover their health.'

'On Honesty's behalf I can recognise the problem,' Jack said. 'In big farming operations, the personal touch between a stockman and his animals is often lost. Sadly over the past few decades all governments have supported and encouraged ever larger establishments, whether they be farms or hospitals. "Best use of resources and technology" and "efficiency" are cited as the reasons to promote large scale operations, but the small scale advantages of relationship, and identity with individuals and locality are lost in the process.'

The doctor and the sister agreed. 'We are hoping that as our MP, Honesty will urge the Government to retain our cottage hospitals,' the doctor said.

'I will definitely do my best,' Jack replied. 'It is something I'm sure that Honesty can relate to.'

'Perhaps you could bring Honesty out of the trailer,' the sister said. 'We have all been looking forward to seeing her. We have arranged for those patients that cannot get out of bed to be moved to a position where they can see her.'

Jack returned to the trailer and, attaching the rope to Honesty's halter, he led her across the car park and onto the lawn. The nurses had opened the French windows and wheeled some of the beds out onto the veranda, while other staff and patients gathered around to see her. Honesty sniffed at the lawn, but the grass was too short to graze. However, as Jack led her past a rose bed, she paused and pulled on the halter rope sufficiently to enable her to wrap her tongue around a few leaves as she sauntered past.

'No, Honesty!' Jack said, embarrassed by her bad manners, which caused a deal of merriment among her audience.

'Animals are particularly important to many patients' well being,' the sister said. 'At some hospitals small animals are brought in for patients, particularly children and the elderly, to hold and caress. There appears to be something comforting about stroking an animal that helps the healing process.'

'I can understand that,' Jack said. 'I have worked with cows all my life. I can confirm that there is something about the presence of animals that is soothing, especially when they are relaxed. I only wish that more people could visit and relate to farm animals. There is so much potential for benefit on both sides from such an interaction.'

One of the patients had gone to his locker and returned with a bunch of grapes. 'Would she like some grapes?' he asked.

'I'm sure she would,' Jack grinned, taking the grapes and offering some to Honesty. She opened her mouth and took them. Having savoured them, she looked back at the remainder of the bunch hopefully.

Photographs were taken before Honesty was returned to her trailer and the patients to their wards.

'Thank you for bringing her,' the sister said.

'It is our pleasure,' Jack replied.

~

Over the next few weeks of summer, Jack and Honesty visited residential homes caring for elderly and handicapped people. Each time it seemed that Honesty's presence was very much appreciated by the seniors and disabled people. Jack would sometimes receive touching letters later, telling how they had felt better following her visit.

'If one heifer can make such a difference, to even just a few people, just imagine what a difference a whole herd would make,' Beth once remarked.

'Honesty hasn't been able to influence any decision making in Parliament yet, but I'm sure she is making a difference to people already,' Jack said to Beth on the way home.

Chapter six

As the new parliamentary session got underway, Jack was pleased to be able to discuss issues that he felt passionately about with people who had influence on decision making. He was particularly concerned by the fact that regulations and laws were not applied even-handedly. Minor infringements would feel the full weight of the law without allowance for mitigating circumstances, while reports of blatant cruelty, very often inherent in factory farm environments were not followed up. Too often the authorities willingly accepted the excuses of the producers and were not prepared to investigate further. It seemed that the most honest and vulnerable were the easiest to intimidate and prosecute.

He was also aware of the staggering incompetence of some government agencies. The stroke of a pen, or lack thereof, could easily bring about bankruptcy, while the perpetrators knew nothing of the effects their unprofessional conduct had had – and cared even less.

Many other MPs and officials were sympathetic to his views on the rural economy and also animal welfare, but at times he found that entrenched attitudes were hard to dispel. He found that there would always be those that considered that farmers had little emotional commitment to their animals. This he also knew from first hand experience was not true of all livestock keepers.

'When you deal with animals on a daily basis you can't help but recognise personalities and inevitably you become attached to individuals, especially those who have served their owners willingly,' he said. 'To bury an animal with respect, on the land where they have lived, is a dignified procedure, but even this is now denied us.'

His companions did not reply. He had found that expressing genuine emotion was as rare as hens teeth among politicians and their associated bureaucrats. He thought of the ill-conceived decisions made on economic and political grounds that had resulted in mass slaughter and the effects that it had had on individual farmers, their families and their communities.

'When a farmer's whole herd or flock are slaughtered en masse without regard to science, let alone sensitivity or sensibility, the whole family can be reduced to tears,' he said bitterly. His companions shifted uncomfortably and the conversation was steered in another direction.

Jack spoke regularly on issues of justice – in debates of both national and international concerns. He always reminded himself of the reasons why people had voted for Honesty. He found that constant reference to the young heifer helped him decide what position he should take. Ethical behaviour and sustainability were all important. He considered how local communities, whether urban or rural, were affected by any proposed legislation and he often found himself voting on her behalf, against the other parties, in the interests of the people.

~

On the day of a debate on farming subsidies Jack felt it was particularly important that Honesty herself should attend the Commons Chamber, as the matter was relevant both to her species, with regard to the animal welfare concerns, and also to many of her constituents. Beth and Jack collected her from the city farm in the afternoon, parked the Land Rover and trailer in the members car park and led her into the building.

'She's bulling, Jack,' Beth had said as she had led Honesty into the trailer.

'Yes,' Jack replied, grimacing 'She's a vocal heifer and she's not going to respect the proceedings in the Commons Chamber at a time like this.'

As they both led Honesty through the corridors towards the Chamber, she was less placid than usual and occasionally pulled on her halter rope. At one point she stopped and, looking around, gave voice to a hearty 'Moo'. Her call reverberated around the august hallway, and passing MPs and officials looked towards her. Although they had become used to seeing her, this was the first time they had heard her give voice. She bawled again. One of the officials came over.

'What's the matter with her?' he enquired.

Jack pursed his lips. 'She's bulling,' he said.

'She's what?'

'She's bulling – she's on heat.'

The official looked at her with concern. 'What does that mean?' he said.

'It just means that she will call and be a bit agitated for a few hours,' Jack explained.

'She's not likely to cause any problems in the Chamber, is she?' the official continued uncertainly.

'No, I shouldn't think so,' Jack said, glancing at Beth.

Jack installed Honesty in her pen. She shifted about in the straw and didn't settle to eat as she normally did. The benches filled up as the other MPs entered and settled down in their accustomed places. The MP who was to speak on the subject rose from his seat.

'On the issue of subsidies for small scale farming it must be borne in mind that efficiency is of particular importance. Although subsidies are to be granted for environmental work, when it comes to producing food we must remember that we operate in a global economy and all technical and scientific applications must be grasped and administered if we are to remain competitive. In this day and age we cannot afford to look back towards an imagined Arcadia of buxom milkmaids. If we are to be competitive then we must intensify all methods of production and if that means industrial livestock units then that must be the case.'

Jack looked at the MP, a large blustering man. He had seen him about before, and had instinctively felt that he did not like Honesty. When their paths had crossed in the corridors the large man had shown no friendliness towards the young farmer.

Jack caught the eye of the Speaker, and rose to respond.

'As the human spokesman for the member for Leythorpe Valley,' he said. 'I must respond to the Honourable Member's remarks about intensive farming. High animal welfare standards must be adhered to whatever the size of the farm. Increasing individual production compromises welfare, and factory farm methods lead to outbreaks of disease, affecting animals and birds and subsequently the food. Small scale producers need the benefits of their less intensive methods to be recognised and supported.' Honesty shifted about in her pen. 'Also all production, whether livestock or crops, must take place with due regard for the health of the soil. There are important issues of sustainability of both land and communities involved, and these cannot be dismissed simply by referring to the global economy.'

The large MP rose to speak again. 'Mr Speaker, the Honourable Member's representative has a natural concern for animal welfare but he clearly does not appreciate the necessity for efficient food production – and if that means the animals and birds can no longer live in an imagined Eden of Arcadian agriculture then that must be the case. Subsidies to cushion the uneconomic end of the livestock sector are an indulgence that we cannot afford.'

Jack felt the anger rising within him. What did this man know of the difficulties facing farming families and the resulting impact on animal welfare. When had this man got up in the middle of the night to assist an animal giving birth, and the emotions felt by all members of the family when, despite their hard work, their income could not match their expenditure.

Honesty, who up till then had been moving about in her pen impatiently, suddenly gave voice to her frustrations. 'Mooooo,' she bawled. Jack stood up to try and calm her, but Honesty would have none of it.

'Moooo,' she called again. She had certainly got the attention of the House.

'Mooo,' some of the MPs replied, encouraging her.

'Order, order,' the Speaker shouted. 'Would the Honourable Member for Leythorpe Valley please refrain from calling in this manner.'

'Mooo,' shouted Honesty again to the accompaniment of the other MPs.

The Speaker now addressed Jack. 'Is there some problem with the cow?' he said.

'No, no problem,' Jack replied.

'Then why does she keep mooing?' the speaker enquired exasperatedly.

'She's bulling – she's calling for a bull,' Jack explained.

At this the House erupted in a crescendo of shouting, laughter and mooing as the MPs rose from their seats waving their order papers.

'Order! Order!' shrieked the Speaker.

'Moooo,' bawled Honesty and the MPs bellowed their enthusiastic response.

Jack gazed around him in amazement. He had been prepared for noisy and sometimes irreverent behaviour, but the juvenile response of some of these people, elected to represent their constituents in the imposing surroundings of such an historic building, surprised him. After all, Honesty was only displaying her natural behaviour – but then perhaps these men and women were also just doing that, too.

Jack glanced towards the Prime Minister, who was looking towards him whilst in conversation with the Home Secretary, amid all the tumult. Jack knew this would bode no good. He knew that the Prime Minister, who had previously spoken to Honesty with a fixed smile on his face, would like to see her removed from Parliament. When the House had quietened down, the speeches continued. Honesty still fidgeted, but her occasional calls no longer attracted the same attention.

The large MP continued to speak of the economic benefits of industrial scale livestock farming, showing little regard for animal or human welfare, and Jack responded.

~

The following afternoon there was a vote on the issue. All the MPs rose to adjourn to the voting lobbies and Jack attached the rope to Honesty's halter. The large MP had left the Chamber ahead of them, but had been required to attend to an urgent call before he had been able to cast his vote.

During that afternoon Honesty had been more contented than she had the previous day, and had lain down chewing her cud throughout the session. Now required to attend the voting lobby with Jack, she had stretched leisurely and followed behind the other MPs. Jack always kept her at the back of any crush of people as it put less stress on both of them. But the previous episode of cudding, combined with the present exercise, had activated Honesty's digestive system, and as they made their way towards the voting lobby, she paused and gazing placidly into space, raised her tail.

'Not now Honesty, *please*,' he said anxiously. He looked around him, usually one of his assistants were in attendance with the bucket, shovel and bag of sawdust, when he and Honesty moved through the building - but today there was nobody about.

'Come on, Jack, you'll miss the vote if you don't hurry up,' one of the other MPs called.

'I'll clear that up in a moment,' Jack said to passers by, who were carefully side stepping the offending dollop.

'Hey, wait for me,' a voice suddenly shouted.

The large MP who had spoken so adamantly on the need for industrial farming with its associated detrimental effect on animal welfare, ran towards the lobby entrance anxious to cast his vote. With seconds to spare it seemed he would reach the doors in time - but suddenly his feet went from under him. There was a thud, some verbal obscenities and moments later he recovered his feet, his suit liberally covered with bovine excrement, as Honesty and Jack walked into the voting lobby and the doors closed behind them.

Chapter seven

After they had voted, Jack returned Honesty to her pen. The other members slowly returned to the Chamber and a short while later, officials returned with the result of the vote. A cheer went up from those who, like Jack, had voted to improve economic conditions for small-scale producers, and against creating favourable conditions for more industrial scale agribusiness. Jack glanced at Honesty in the pen beside him, and grinned at her. This was what he had hoped for when he had accepted her election as MP.

Later that evening, after he had attended to Honesty, Jack went to one of the local bars, where members of the Westminster staff often gathered for informal conversation and refreshment. He bought a drink and some sandwiches and seated himself at one of the tables.

'May I join you?' a smartly dressed man, aged about 60 years, sat down opposite Jack.

'You speak very well,' he said. 'I like the points you make in your speeches.'

'I interpret Honesty's thoughts,' Jack said with a smile.

'Quite so,' his companion replied. 'I am a friend of Jim Drury.'

'Pleased to meet you,' Jack said. 'Mr Drury has been very helpful and I very much appreciate his support.'

'Honesty's election caused a real stir here, not just because she was a cow,' the man said. 'The people had voted for change, for truth and honesty, not a false façade of empty words. The leaders of all parties fear that that idea may spread. The Government is rushing through legislation to prevent any more animals being elected, they cannot risk any more animals with names like Truth, Justice and Sincerity being elected, this would raise awareness of how little relevance these things have in Parliament these days. Too many people have too much to lose if both Government and Opposition act honestly and ethically. They need the present system - in which opposing debate is seemingly encouraged, while the real issues and influences are obscured.'

'I could see that people were cynical of politicians from what they said when I was canvassing with Honesty, and with good reason it seems,' Jack said.

'Genuine statesmen are rare nowadays,' the man continued. 'The pursuit of power, status and the attendant economic advantages overrides inconveniences like conscience and honesty. All parties operate policies which take advantage of short term gains. The long term effects of these policies are ignored. Elected representatives voting with their conscience are regarded as a hindrance in the Party political system, and within global economics it is regarded as a weakness. Manipulation in the drive for power and control is regarded as strength.'

Jack already had experience of this in regard to the supermarkets.

'Honesty has no wish for power, she wants to empower individuals,' Jack said.

'That is what is so refreshing about her election,' the man replied. 'But the players behind the scenes of the global stage exert more influence than you would imagine.

'Both corporations and governments desire control,' he continued. 'And they are not beyond directing events in their own interests. Secrecy is essential and money buys silence. Big money buys a lot of silence. Sometimes fear is used to encourage people to accept something that in other circumstances they would reject. The media is concerned with hype and sensationalism – raising fears without any investigation. Facts, that do not fit the message or impression that is being conveyed, are suppressed or ignored. If something is repeated often enough it will be believed, even though its veracity has never been confirmed. Manipulation is endemic – whether it be of the media, of situations, or of the people.' The man paused. 'Sometimes the manipulation is subtle - over a number of years - until it is so widely accepted that the people don't realise that they are being deceived. At other times it is more blatant, with disinformation cast about like confetti.'

'I have already come to realise that national politics are too often influenced by other factors to faithfully represent the best interests of the people,' Jack admitted, although he was rather taken aback at what this man was saying.

'Of course,' the man replied. 'Transnational corporations and international financial institutions operate a global policy and national governments are caught up in this. Self-sufficiency, whether it be local food production or indigenous tribal groups are an anathema to them. There are "inducements" to follow a certain route, or to refrain from taking others. The vanity and arrogance of many political leaders play into their hands. Some countries suffer considerably more than others, but none are immune.'

Jack thought of what the South American Ambassador had said to him a few months ago. He had assumed that he was only referring to Third World countries, but this man was saying otherwise.

'Where policies are introduced that do not appear to be in the best interests of the country or the people,' the man said, 'always think *"cui bono?"* - who benefits? The answer will invariably indicate why a particular policy decision was taken. You are taking on Goliath, Jack,' he continued. 'It's not just one or two self-seeking individuals you are up against. The politicians and the people are manipulated. There are other players in the game. Nothing is as it seems.'

'I hadn't realised the extent of the deception,' Jack said.

The man rose from his seat. 'The fact that I am talking to you now will have been noted,' he said with a wry smile. 'Honesty's election has made people take notice. She has provided the opportunity for them to take note of things they probably haven't considered before.'

The man left and Jack held his glass in his hands. He thought about what the man had said - and what had happened over the past few years. He also thought of the recent mass slaughter of farm animals - the majority of them healthy - of threats and intimidation, unlawful entry and use of force. Why? He wondered if reports of the use of the Official Secrets Act at that time, had any connection with what this man was saying. The Government had subsequently passed legislation, which indicated that they had known they were acting unlawfully at the time. Very often he felt he wanted to be back on the farm, driving the tractor, doing physical work again. He was much happier out there than amid all the duplicity and deceit in the capital. He finished his drink and got up and returned to the flat.

~

Jack's busy schedule continued unabated. He welcomed genuine radio and television debates, but he was less keen on the presenters who regarded Honesty's election as an extended publicity stunt.

Beth was as busy as ever with piles of paperwork.

'The amount of letters we have is unbelievable,' she said. 'It is amazing how many things people are writing to us about - not only to do with farming and animals, but anything involving perceived injustice and dishonesty in local as well as national government. We've also had letters from people offering to sponsor her for charity events,' she continued, as Jack signed several letters on Honesty's behalf.

'But we can hardly expect her to do a sponsored parachute jump,' Jack said.

'No, but you could,' Beth replied. Jack did not look confident.

'I'd rather do something that is more relevant to Honesty herself,' he said. 'You know, something like a "Ragwort Pull" - dried ragwort is poisonous to animals when it is fed to them in their hay - or a "Litter Pick" - litter can be dangerous to livestock and wildlife, as well as being unsightly.'

Later that day they visited Honesty at the city farm. She came over to them.

'You're gorgeous,' Jack said, scratching the top of her head. She repaid the complement by extending her tongue and wrapping it around the side of his face in a gesture of affection.

'You know, Beth,' he said. 'I don't think either the voters or myself had any idea the effect Honesty was going to have. All those letters and the phone calls. I never thought a heifer, even with a name like Honesty, could activate such previously undisclosed thoughts and feelings. It's as if she had made people wake up.'

'I'm sure most of them would not have written to a human MP,' Beth replied. 'It is as if they think she will listen, where another person won't.'

'Perhaps it's something to do with her big ears,' Jack said, grinning, as Honesty's black tipped ears turned like antennae to catch the conversation.

Chapter eight

On a Monday morning of the autumn term, Jack drove to an agricultural college in the Midlands. He had been asked to speak to a gathering of students and graduates on his views of farm animal welfare and it's effects on the economy. He took Honesty along, as her presence would reinforce anything he said concerning animal welfare.

He was met at the main entrance and shown to a large open pen in one of the farm buildings. Honesty was led into the pen, which she walked around approvingly. Already quite a crowd of students and tutors had gathered around. Her fame, which was the envy of many an aspiring celebrity, drew crowds normally reserved for prize-winning cows and the dams of high-ranking bulls. Honesty's status was unique.

'Welcome Jack,' the principal said, offering the usual hospitality to a visiting speaker. 'We have been looking forward to seeing you. We have seen so much of you and Honesty in the media, it is a great privilege to have you here as our guest.'

'Thank you for the invitation,' Jack said. 'I feel so much more comfortable here in a farming environment than I ever do in the House. Here, we understand each other. There, some of Honesty's fellow MPs have no understanding of farming or life outside a big city.'

The audience had taken their places and the Principal introduced Jack, who stepped forward.

'I am very pleased to be here to be able to address you personally on matters, that as Honesty's spokesman, are of great concern to all of us. The rural economy is still very much dependant on farming, despite the recent increase in recreational activities in the countryside. For farming, particularly livestock farming, to be regarded with the respect it deserves from consumers, high animal welfare is of utmost importance. We cannot deny that some disreputable people compromise animal welfare for profit. That is not acceptable. It creates a bad image of farmers in general, linking the good with the bad.'

Jack spoke eloquently on all the aspects of animal husbandry, the link with the local community and consumers.

'Honesty has been a goodwill ambassador for her species,' he said. 'Her election has enabled people to relate to her. She is not just a production unit, they recognise her as a representative of another species, in many ways not so dissimilar to their own companion animals. When they meet her, there is a subtle interaction. After such an encounter people do not want to hear of animals being abused in industrialised factory farms. They vote with their purses and wallets and pay to shop where they know the animals have been well treated. Subsequently the producer receives a fair return and the local economy benefits.'

Jack was applauded at the end of his speech and he then invited questions from the audience. The supermarkets were targeted for much complaint, as their price wars drove down the prices paid to producers. The Government also came in for equal criticism, from the innumerable regulations and bureaucracy affecting all aspects of livestock and arable farming, to the heavy handed insensitivity of it's agencies.

Jack was reminded of what Mr Drury had said, not only about so many laws and regulations being made outside Westminster, but also that those same regulations were enforced with added vigour by the officials of the ministries concerned. Sometimes it seemed that officialdom, whether political, civil or even scientific were out to create burdens and injustices where none need ever exist.

Other times it seemed that no sooner had one animal disease scare threatened the demise of livestock farming, than another scare or disease took its place. Independent investigation could well reveal that bad practice and a disregard for welfare in large factory systems had led to problems. But a media addicted to hyperbole and graphic images, appeared reluctant to report that less stress in organic and extensive systems meant less disease. Jack had already noted that when the Government sought recommendations from advisory committees, there was no enquiry as to whether the members of these committees had a conflict of interest, or if the organisations they represented were dependent on industry funding. It was rumoured that funding was often dependent on the researchers producing the desired result.

'Unsubstantiated claims of risks to human health are broadcast on the authority of individuals without being verified by peer reviewed science,' Jack said. 'But where other scientific investigation refutes these claims, the researchers are ridiculed and their findings are withheld. Enormous sums of public money are expended in being seen to counteract perceived risks, while the true cause of distressing and sometimes fatal diseases are not properly investigated. Thousands of healthy animals also pay the ultimate sacrifice for poor science, conjecture and inappropriate pronouncements.'

'Have you been contacted by farm animal welfare campaigners?' Jack was asked.

'Yes, I have,' he replied. 'Their contact with me has been polite, and we agree that high animal welfare is of utmost importance. It should not just be a superficial marketing ploy. Intensive production, either by breeding or by housing, impacts badly on the welfare of animals and poultry. This issue must be addressed not only by the farmers, but also by the consumers and the prices they are prepared to pay.

In many ways it is all down to respect – respect for the living animal, throughout its life and at the time of slaughter – and respect for food in the kitchen and on the table. Wasted food is disrespect to all concerned in its production – including the animals. Over the years people have lost their connection with the land. If people connect with Honesty, they will care about how their food is produced and act accordingly.'

'What of those people who advocate a vegetarian diet?' another questioner remarked.

'Yes, there are some who hold the opinion that animals should not be farmed at all. I respect their views although personally I do not agree with them.' Jack paused.

'With a basic need for food,' he continued, 'there would have to be an increase in arable crops, which unless it were organic, would be treated several times a year with pesticide applications. These chemical cocktails have been linked with many health problems. Without animal manure the condition of the soil deteriorates, as the microbes necessary for a healthy soil are lost. This has been admirably illustrated in Third World countries where farmers have been provided with livestock. The productivity of their land has increased enormously where the animal dung improves fertility. Although green manures also increase fertility, personally I like to see animals grazing in the fields and on the hills. Where animals have been lost from the land there is an emptiness, it has lost its vitality.'

'How do you think bad practises should be dealt with?' another questioner asked.

'As I mentioned before, the purchasing power of consumers is all important,' Jack replied. 'But as that is unlikely to take place overnight, I think there is a necessity for the regulatory authorities to take action in cases of cruelty and welfare issues that are reported to them. Too often they accept excuses and fail to investigate further, or to prosecute. Such failures can lead to suspicion that they were influenced by financial interests. We are all losers, not only the animals, but also our faith in the integrity of the administrators.'

Another questioner raised her hand. 'What are your thoughts on the distance animals have to travel to slaughter?' she asked.

'That is something I am very much concerned with,' Jack replied. 'Up until a few years ago there was an abattoir in a small town only eight miles from our farm. We had visited the premises and knew that the stress our animals were put under was reduced to the minimum. However because of new directives, many of which were inappropriate for such a small business, the proprietor was forced to close down. Now our animals have to be transported a much greater distance to a larger concern. We know it creates more stress for our animals and we wish there was an alternative, but until our elected Westminster MPs, of whom Honesty is one, can regain control of the legislative process we will continue to be subjected to these directives.'

After the vote of thanks, Jack mingled with members of the audience.

'As the son of a dairy farmer,' he said, 'I have always known that cows have personalities, but since I have had such a close connection to Honesty, I realise how much she trusts me. As well as providing food, water and shelter, she trusts me to do her no harm. I now recognise that all animals have that same need to trust - although sadly that trust is too often misplaced,' he confided.

Later Jack and several of the students went out to the barn where Honesty had spent the time ruminating, while her spokesman had been presenting her views. They had previously only seen her as a heifer, albeit a bovine celebrity rather than a working animal, but following Jack's speech they had a new comprehension of her role as the focus of Jack's position in Parliament As Jack represented them, so Honesty was representative of their own stock.

Jack attached the rope to her halter.

'Farm animals have an understanding few people realise,' he said. Honesty fidgeted, moving her head up and down, as if nodding in agreement, a gesture which was not lost on one or two of those present including Jack himself. His reception by his peers had been successful. The audience had recognised his sincerity, as had the voters of Leythorpe Valley, when they voted for honesty and integrity in the shape of a Holstein heifer.

Chapter nine

Springtime is always welcome after the winter months, but in the countryside, in which for centuries work had been regulated by the seasonal clock, the signs are noticed first by those who work outdoors.

After a successful grant application, Mr Watson had employed a local craftsman to lay the hedges around some of the fields during the winter. Some new whips had been planted in gaps in the old hedgerows and a new spinney created. The Watsons had farmed their land for four generations and had retained many features which, due to changes in farming practices and lack of environmental concern, had resulted in their removal on many other holdings.

Jack remembered when his father had brought out an old map of the farm. It showed where present day footpaths had once been important routes between neighbouring villages, and even the site of former dwellings now barely recognised as uneven ground at the edge of a field. John Watson was a practical modern farmer, but he remembered the hours of enjoyment he had had around the farm when he was a boy and wanted future generations to have the same opportunities. He modernised as far as was necessary, but he liked the old barns and byres, where he stored one or two old implements, and refused to have the cobble stones on the far side of the present farmyard concreted over.

'It's part of our history,' he would say, 'I don't want my grandchildren knowing how things were just from books and photographs.'

But as farming incomes had reduced, his decisions had to be influenced by a tighter budget.

Jack, like his father, had played around the farm as a boy. He knew where the first frogspawn could be found, where the different birds nested, which trees were best for climbing. Up until his unexpected move to Westminster he had been a partner with his father in running the herd and the farm. Both father and son appreciated the value of landscape features, and took advice on how these could be developed. The two ponds on the farm, which had once been the source of drinking water for the livestock were still maintained, though the cattle now drank from galvanised troughs in the fields.

The Watsons had not uprooted their hedges as many arable farmers had done in the middle of the twentieth century. They recognised them as windbreaks for the animals to shelter behind. In particular Jack liked the mature trees that dotted the hedgerows. On very hot summer days the cattle would seek the shade, the dominant animals selecting the best spots, while the lower ranks of the herd remained on the edge of the shadow.

'People often tell me that the rural economy and farming in particular have got to move with the times,' Jack said to his father. 'They don't see that a thriving and diverse rural environment is as important to national culture as the National Gallery.'

'Food production is a priority land use,' his father replied. 'But I agree, farmland devoted to crop production must be balanced with areas of fallow, where native plant and animal species can survive - we need both.'

'Granddad had to do as the agricultural advisors told him in the Second World War because food production was essential,' Jack said. 'Nowadays it's not regarded with the same importance. They say we can buy it cheaper from abroad.'

'It's a short sighted policy,' Mr Watson replied. 'Several farms around here have been sold over the past twelve months and the buildings converted. If food imports fail for any reason, which can happen all too easily, you can't suddenly start producing enough food to feed the nation when the skills and infrastructure have gone.'

'The global economy has destroyed the traditional mixed farm,' Jack said. 'Villages have lost their sense of community as many interdependent little businesses have closed. There used to be three pubs in the village up to a few years ago, now there's only one.'

'In that case,' his father said, slapping Jack on the shoulders, 'I think it's about time we supported the Dun Cow before it succumbs to global economics.'

~

Jack checked his diary for the next day. He had the monthly surgery in Honesty's constituency to attend, he was booked to visit a local junior school, and he had arranged to have lunch with a local farmers leader.

Jack liked attending schools, unlike a lot of other politicians, who were predominantly interested in promoting the policies of their party.

The teachers often found imaginative ways to involve Honesty's election into the various subjects that the children were learning. The schools usually asked that he should bring Honesty with him. She was a great favourite with most of the children, although some were initially intimidated by her size. On the whole she was placid and amenable on these visits and invariably won over the most nervous child. Occasionally he had been asked to visit inner city schools where the children had been amazed by Honesty's appearance. Many of them had no knowledge of farming or farm animals. She was usually the largest animal they had met.

'Do you ride her?' one boy enquired of Jack.

'No people don't ride cows,' he replied.

'Then what do you keep them for?' the boy asked, puzzled..

When Jack spoke to the children he varied what he said depending on the age of the classes. With the younger children he compared Honesty's requirements to those of their pets at home. He explained how farmers looked after cows and other farm animals, and the necessity to ensure that they were well cared for. The teachers encouraged the children to do drawings of her.

With the older children, Jack would speak about how Honesty came to be elected, the meaning of her names, and how he spoke on her behalf at Westminster. The teachers would ask the children to write what their dogs and cats and rabbits and hamsters would do and say if they were elected to Parliament. Sometimes the teachers would ask Jack to judge what they had written.

He would show some of these little compositions to Beth.

'These children have a far greater understanding and sensitivity than many adults, particularly most politicians,' he said. 'It is very encouraging when you consider that they are the future citizens, and everything is eventually going to depend on their choices and decisions.'

Beth read what they had written. 'They write about kindness not only towards animals but also between people. Their references to peace is remarkable, few adults asked to write about animals or elected representatives would mention that.'

~

The following morning the head teacher greeted Jack, when he arrived. The school covered a rural area, so many of the children were already familiar with farm animals.

'My dad said he wants to get our bull elected next time,' one boy told Jack, who could well imagine how the rest of the conversation had gone.

'We try to involve the children's own situations in the things that we teach,' the head mistress told him. 'Whenever possible we go out into the countryside and relate what we see there to whatever task the children are working on at the time. There have been rumours that it is the intention of the Education Authority to close this and some other village schools,' she continued. 'We are all very concerned about this. The children benefit so much from being in a small school. If they have to travel to a bigger school, it is the local authority who gains, not the children or their parents.'

'These small rural schools are very important,' Jack said. 'They are essential to the countryside communities that I support as Honesty's spokesman.'

'We have already explained to the children about Honesty being elected to represent the people in this area,' the headmistress said. 'They wanted to meet her and put questions to her, perhaps you can interpret her replies for us.'

Jack smiled, 'I'll do my best.'

One girl put her hand up. She addressed Honesty, 'What do you most like about being a Member of Parliament?' she asked.

Jack looked at the heifer. 'I understand that she likes her comfortable pen in the House of Commons, which is well supplied with hay and straw,' he said. 'And as a Member of Parliament she also likes being able to help people, through me, who ask for her assistance.'

'What do you most dislike about being an MP?' another boy asked.

Again Jack turned towards Honesty. 'She most dislikes having to listen to long speeches by other MPs,' he said. 'But if they become too tedious, she lies down and chews her cud.'

At the end of the question and answer session, the head mistress asked Jack if they could have Honesty's signature, to append to the displays that they had put on the classroom walls.

'We have prepared some paint soaked sponges in the

playground,' she explained. 'If we could ask you to lead Honesty across them and then onto some sheets of paper, I think we should get some reasonable signatures.' Jack thought it was an excellent idea and Honesty obligingly stepped onto the sponges and across the paper, leaving the desired hoof prints in red and green paint.

The headmistress thanked Jack. 'We have never asked a Member of Parliament to our school before,' she said. 'We have been able to learn so much in preparation for your visit, and the children and the staff have really enjoyed meeting you both.'

Jack loaded Honesty back into the trailer, and the children and teachers waved goodbye as they drove off down the road.

~

After he had left the school, Jack drove to the home of the local farmers leader. He drove into the yard and two noisy dogs came out to greet him.

'Hello there,' a middle aged man walked across the yard. He came to the door of the Land Rover. 'I'll show you where to park, you can unload Honesty, then you must come in for a cup of tea. Lunch will be ready shortly.'

Jack parked the vehicle and lowered the ramp of the trailer.

'Let's take a look at this famous lady then,' the man said. Jack led Honesty out. 'She'll make a good milker,' he remarked looking her up and down. 'Or do you intend her to make a career out of politics?'

'It's good to meet you,' the man said as he poured the tea. 'I've seen some of what you've said in the farming press, but they tend to be flippant about you.'

'I know,' Jack replied. 'The official farmers representatives have avoided me. They gave me no support when Honesty entered Parliament. They just regarded us a gimmick.'

The man nodded. 'Perhaps they are too cosy with agribusiness and the Establishment. Anyway our members around here appreciate what you are doing.'

The farmer pushed a pile of papers across the table to make room for their plates.

'I don't know if anyone realises the amount of paperwork involved in every aspect of farming these days,' he said. 'But even though we will fill in all these forms we are no better off, in fact we are worse off. Some weeks ago one of our members applied to move some of his cows and calves from a restricted zone. They were desperately short of grazing and the wet weather had made the conditions appalling. Yet despite his repeated letters and phone calls, the department never replied or gave him the permission he needed. They seem indifferent to the suffering they are inflicting.'

'A few weeks ago, some of our members gathered outside a local supermarket,' the farmer continued as they ate their meal. 'We wanted to let shoppers know how little the supermarket was paying us - in some cases below the cost of production. There was no disorderly conduct, but somebody must have called the police.' He paused. 'They took photographs of us,' he said. 'I don't understand why peaceful demonstrators should be treated as if they are a threat to the nation.'

'You may not be a threat to the nation, but you could be considered a threat to corporate profits,' Jack replied. 'It is the corporate chemical, scientific and technical assault that has the greatest potential to destroy lives and livelihoods throughout the world that particularly bothers me,' he continued. 'For many years now many cattle in North America have had to suffer the intrusive application of drugs on a regular basis to increase milk production. This inevitably impacts badly on the welfare of the cows, with unknown consequences for the consumers of that milk. This is a misuse of science and a totally unacceptable method of increasing profits. Further pressure from the corporations has prevented consumers from exercising their choice as to whether or not to buy the milk, although the drug is banned here in Britain.'

Later as they walked around the farm looking at the stock, they discussed the apparent discrepencies between the official voice of farming and the views held by many family farmers.

'When it comes to animal disease, there's too much reliance on academic theory,' the farmer said. 'Also, the media fail to point out that not all animal diseases affect human beings - Foot and Mouth for instance. Do people realise that the mass slaughter during the FMD outbreak was for political and economic reasons? There was no risk to human beings. FMD is not fatal to animals either - if they are suffering then perhaps slaughter is the best option, but many animals recover completely - and with the right preventative measures they may well avoid becoming infected in the first place. Our members have got practical experience going back over generations, but the Ministry won't listen to them.'

Jack thought about the academics who had made statements that had caused devastation to whole sectors of livestock farming, without consideration of the effects their words would have. It seemed beyond comprehension that they were unaware of the likely consequences of their remarks.

'I know,' Jack replied. 'Millions of pounds have been spent implementing policies that rely on a preferred theory, without seeking investigation or other advice. It doesn't make sense.'

'I suppose "sense" depends on what the long term plan is,' the farmer remarked.

~

With his heavy workload, Jack had had little opportunity

to socialise with the friends who had helped get Honesty elected.

'How does it feel to be employed by a cow?' one of them asked when he at last met up with them.

'It feels fine,' he said, grinning 'Actually we are a team. Neither of us could operate without the other.' He bought a round of drinks and they all gathered around one of the tables.

'Tell us what it's like there then?' another one said.

'Nothing like the real practical work I'm used to,' he said. 'Lots of talking, lots of paper, but when it comes to initiating policies which should be for the common good, it seems they are directed more towards the benefit of the few.'

'People wouldn't have voted for Honesty if they felt that politicians acted in their best interests,' one of his companions noted casually.

'That's right,' Jack replied. 'It creates distrust of politicians. For that reason people find Honesty's humility a refreshing change.'

'So what's the answer?' one of the girls asked.

'Animal emancipation!' another replied. 'We got Honesty elected last time. Perhaps a few white rabbits may make it next time.'

Jack smiled. 'I sometimes think I am already exploring down a rabbit hole.'

Chapter ten

The following week-end, Jack rang Mr Drury.
'Hello there, how are things at that hothouse of control, self interest and sexual intrigue,' the older man said.

Jack laughed, 'Much as you describe it,' he said. 'But Jim, I rang because I want your advice. Our postbag is still as full as ever, but while Honesty has a seat in Parliament, I need to create informed opinion about things she represents so that others will follow the direction she has pointed.'

'Yes, I can understand that,' Mr Drury replied. 'I know you and Honesty visit as many people and enterprises as you can, but you could do with involving other members in the causes you take up. A good way to do that would be to create an unofficial committee. Invite a selection of other members, covering all the other parties. You could then visit as a group and you would be seen as less of a one man band.'

'Thanks,' Jack said. 'I like that idea. I feel I need to mix more with other members who I know are sympathetic to the issues I raise.'

Over the week-end, Jack mulled over the various concerns he wanted to highlight - animal welfare, farming and the rural economy and the environment. As they drove back to London on the Monday morning, Jack discussed Mr Drury's suggestion with Beth.

'Well there are no shortage of places you could visit with your committee,' she said. 'An ideal place would be an organic farm, they incorporate several of the issues you want to highlight.'

'That's right,' Jack said. 'Do we have any organic farms on our list of correspondents.'

'I'm sure we have,' Beth said. 'I'll look some up, when I get to the office, while you can make a start on the committee.'

By that evening, Beth had selected two farms, which she thought would be ideal for the purposes of a visit by the committee. One farm in the Midlands encouraged visitors and was well known in organic farming circles. The other, a family run farm, was in the West Country, and was less well known. The daughter of the family had written to Jack inviting him to visit anytime. She had asked that he bring Honesty along as well, as the family, all enthusiastic supporters of animal welfare, were very attached to all their livestock.

Jack himself had made initial enquiries about an unofficial committee, and had approached various MPs who had spoken supportively about Honesty's representation. Some of them represented West Country constituencies, so the selection of the second farm was particularly suitable.

'Sounds a good idea to me,' one of the MPs Jack had approached was enthusiastic. 'I've spoken myself on organic farming, but although the Minister gives lip service to the idea, organic farming doesn't get the support it deserves. It's not seen as carrying vote winning influence, and it is actually in opposition to the influential big pharma lobbying groups.'

Jack nodded. He was aware of the opposition and apathy involved in promoting organic production. 'If we can get our visit reported in the local press - then the farm, Honesty and myself, and the other local MPs will all get positive coverage,' he said.

Some weeks later the small group of MPs had their first meeting. The members of these unofficial committees enjoyed them as much for their social content as any parliamentary work they might carry out, and Jack felt that it would help him gain contacts and develop friendships within Westminster as well as within the organic farming community. All of the MPs were aware of the benefits they would gain from the publicity associated with their visit and were keen to take part. Beth wrote to the farmer and a date agreeable to all parties was arranged.

~

Their visit coincided with the burgeoning growth of spring. And once they had left the urban areas and the motorways behind them, even the jaded sensitivities of some of the MPs could not help but be moved by the sight of the masses of wild flowers along the lanes.

As they drove down the narrow lanes, bordered by high banks, Jack was reminded of the farming history of this part of the country – the traditional family farms, surrounded by small fields. In so many other parts of the country, small farms had been sold and the land incorporated into larger units. Miles of hedges had been removed to accommodate the increasing size of farm machinery over the past few decades – and although more hedge planting had since taken place, the intimacy of the original pastures had been lost. But here the lie of the land had prevented large scale modernisation and the farms had managed to retain their character along with their small fields and woodland.

As the vehicles pulled up in front of the farmhouse, an attractive young woman came out to meet them.

'Hello there, I'm Julie, I'm so pleased you were able to come,' she said, shaking hands with each representative in turn. 'If you take the trailer round the back,' she said to Jack, 'I'll show you a paddock where you can put Honesty. We have all been looking forward to meeting her.'

By now the young woman's father and brother had joined them and the group followed as Jack drove around and parked beside some old traditional barns. He lowered the ramp and led Honesty out. The young woman immediately went up to her.

'Hello beautiful,' she said, scratching her behind the ears.

'Nobody calls me beautiful and scratches me behind the ears,' one of the other MPs commented.

'Ah, but do you have her charm?' the young woman retorted, smiling. 'We have cows on this farm who absolutely ooze character and contentment,' she enthused. 'We were so pleased when we heard that Honesty had been elected as an MP, it's been long overdue for an animal to hold a formal position where she could represent her own species in the eyes of the world. Anyway, do come in and have something to eat – and we can tell you about our farm, then we will show you around and you can meet some of our animals.'

Throughout the meal the family explained the theory and practice of organic farming. 'We allow our animals, and the poultry, to live in as natural a state as possible,' Julie said, as they tucked in to a feast of organic food. 'We regard ourselves as stewards, caring for the animals and the land. We have farmed by organic principles for many years now and are totally committed to its benefits. We watch how the animals interact among themselves, their family relationships, how they seek out certain parts of the farm or certain foods, depending on their needs. We learn from them and that enables us to be better carers.'

'But are you able to farm profitably?' one of the MPs enquired.

'Yes,' she replied. 'We make enough money to cover our costs and have a reasonably good lifestyle. We all enjoy the way we are farming here, we would not want to compromise our system for profit.'

After some delicious locally made ice cream, the party donned wellington boots and followed Julie and her brother out into the yard. Free range hens roamed about scratching the soil in a search for worms and edible morsels.

'That's something you don't see very often these days,' one of the men commented.

'Sadly, not,' Julie replied, 'most farmers specialise now. It's either livestock or poultry units. A farmer's wife rearing a few hens for eggs and for the table is a thing of the past, most farming wives have got a job in town now.'

Julie pointed out one of the hens, 'That's Eglantine. She used to be a battery hen, but someone rescued her when she was due for slaughter. They were unable to keep her themselves and asked if we could take her. She shivered with nerves and lack of feathers when she arrived, but now that she has recovered she is a real character and every so often she lays us an egg, as a sort of thank you,' Julie smiled.

'Do you think people care about the conditions hens and other farm animals are reared in?' one of the MPs asked.

'Yes, I do,' Julie replied. 'But it is important to bring it to their notice. There will always be those who don't care, but a growing number of people are now asking for free range eggs and organic produce. They have been told about the health and animal welfare issues associated with a lot of intensive production and cheap food, and that has influenced their shopping. And of course there are benefits for their own health.'

As the group walked around the corner of the barn, they noticed Honesty on the far side of her small paddock, with several beef cows on the other side of the fence.

'Oh, it hasn't taken them long to find her,' Julie said. 'Cattle are curious animals. As soon as one of them spotted her, they would all come over.'

'I wonder what they are saying to each other,' one of the MPs said.

'Well, Honesty would certainly have plenty to tell them,' another replied.

Julie laughed, 'I can just imagine our girls' reaction

to what she is telling them. They are proper country yokels compared to a sophisticated city girl like her. It would be "Well I never" and "You did what!" but seriously', she continued, 'I am convinced that all animals have a method of communication that we are unaware of. Here on this farm we observe our animals a lot, to the extent that we can recognise what they are communicating with each other. I don't say "saying to each other", because that would indicate verbal communication, and except in cases like a new mother softly murmuring to her calf, most communication is conveyed without making any sound.'

'So what are they communicating?' one of the party asked.

'It very often has to do with relationships,' Julie replied.

'Like us,' another quipped.

'Yes, quite,' Julie said. 'With our beef cattle, the calves stay with their mothers for many months, unlike dairy cows. The calves have the same needs as, and similar characteristics to, all babies. The adult animals also have individual personalities and respond accordingly. We recognise their individual temperaments and see how it effects their interaction among themselves - between mothers and offspring, between friends and between rivals. I also believe that their recognition of relationships also extends to us, their carers, and it is therefore important that we carry out that duty of care with respect for them as individuals.'

'Are you saying that all animals are like this?' one MP asked.

'Yes, of course,' Julie replied, 'but sadly many farm animals are unable to live in their natural social groups and their behaviour is therefore modified to the conditions in which they are reared.'

'Do you think that your relationship with your animals makes any difference to your farming business?' another asked.

'I think it has a positive effect,' Julie said. 'At the local farmers market we have our regular customers who tell us that they buy our produce because they know the animals have been well cared for. Those people tell their friends and that extends our customer base.'

'Do you think your methods will catch on with other farmers?' Julie was asked.

'I think that would have to be a long term expectation,' she replied. 'But that's not to say it won't happen sooner than we expect. After all who would have thought that a heifer would be elected to Parliament.'

Julie and her brother led the group through a gate and onto a green lane bordered by high hedges.

'These parts of the farm are just as important as the grass leys and the arable crops,' she said. 'As a family we have always tried to preserve these mini wildernesses. Some parts are accessible to the cattle and sheep, it gives them the chance to browse other vegetation, but we like to maintain a variety of habitats for other animals and birds. Our farming is as much about quality as quantity.'

'Do other people have access to your land?' Jack asked.

'Yes,' she replied. 'We have a right of way crossing one side of the farm and we have extended it into a nature trail. We have been in touch with local schools to invite them to use it. We have considered other educational developments, but not put them into practice as yet.'

'Your farm would be an excellent educational resource,' Jack said. 'I have found that children and teachers are interested in Honesty – and through her I am able to interest them in other aspects of farming and the countryside.'

'Honesty is a Goodwill Ambassador,' Julie said, echoing Jack's own opinion. 'Ideally we should have a goodwill ambassador of every species. In fact I think we could provide a few from this farm, couldn't we.' She looked at her brother and he smiled his assent.

In one of the adjoining fields a flock of sheep were grazing, but one animal was head and shoulders above the rest. Members of the party stared at it.

'Oh I see you have noticed Cesar, our llama,' Julie said. 'We keep him to protect the flock - he chases off foxes and the like. We much prefer his presence to any other method of pest control.'

Julie and her brother guided the group of MPs through a small woodland, identifying the trees.

'Local naturalists have done surveys here and told us of all the species they have found,' Julie said. 'They have told us that the lack of chemical use has greatly increased the diversity.' The group walked alongside a stream of crystal clear water, bounded by willows and alder, and made their way back towards the farmhouse.

In the kitchen Julie's mother had a large kettle boiling ready to serve cups of tea, together with plates piled with of homemade cakes and biscuits.

'Organic production is no longer seen as a specialist market,' Julie's brother said. 'There are many factors which influence the way the farmer produces his crop or rears his livestock. More often than not sons and daughters continue with the conventional methods that their fathers have used, and those methods are very much what is taught in the farming colleges. There has been a resistance to change, but now there is a recognition that people are concerned about the way that their food is produced, and farming methods must adapt to respond to that. At the most fundamental level the health of the soil itself must be maintained, or restored - this will transfer into healthy crops and healthy animals.'

Julie and her mother passed round the cups of tea.

'But it's not just a matter of physical health,' Julie said. We are now considering using biodynamic methods. That is a natural progression for us. It is taking working with nature a step further forward, using systems that have shown their worth since Rudolf Steiner introduced them in the 1920s.'

'The ethics of livestock production is very important to us,' she continued handing round the plates of biscuits and cakes. 'That is why we have been so pleased that you and Honesty have been able to visit us. I'm sure that she has been learning a lot from her conversations with our animals today and that she strongly approves of what we are doing here. What we would ask is that wherever possible you endorse our methods of production and care.'

Jack looked around his colleagues. 'I'm sure I speak for all of us when I say that we have been most impressed with what we have seen today. As Honesty's spokesman you may rest assured that I will promote your farming methods. particularly the respect in which you hold your livestock.' The others nodded their agreement. Thanking the family for their hospitality, they collected Honesty and returned to London.

Chapter eleven

Jack drove the Land Rover and trailer into the farmyard. It was good to be back in familiar surroundings, helping on the farm and sharing meals with his parents.

After a particularly stressful week, he was more reserved than normal.

'I sometimes wonder where farming will be in 10 years time,' Mr Watson remarked, enjoying a hearty Sunday lunch. 'Every time you think things can't get much worse, something else happens. Maybe not a full blown crisis, but just another nail in the coffin.'

'I've thought about that myself,' Jack said. 'There's been so much happened over the past 20 years or so, I can't help wondering.'

'Wondering what?' his father said.

Jack looked at his plate. 'I've tried to make sense of it all – all the scares, all the slaughter and sensationalism – but investigation is not encouraged as it should be. Official enquiries invariably vindicate the action which was taken, no matter how destructive, and no senior figures are held to account.'

His father didn't reply straight away.

'I think I know what you mean,' he said eventually. 'A few years ago I wouldn't have said that, I'd have just put it down to incompetence, or city folks not understanding the basics of good animal husbandry and food production.'

'That's what I thought too when I first starting campaigning with Honesty,' Jack said. 'Perhaps it sounds crazy, but I sometimes wonder if there isn't another agenda that nobody really knows about.' He paused. 'A few years ago there were credible reports of preparations being made for mass slaughter weeks before the first case of disease was notified, combustible materials ordered – that sort of thing. Why didn't they vaccinate? It was almost as if all the slaughter was meant to happen.'

Mr Watson nodded. 'I remember when we produced the meat and milk that our land could comfortably support,' he said. 'The supply and demand were in balance, as were the methods of production. Then thanks to political meddling, there was overproduction. When restrictions on production were imposed, the calculations were biased against the British dairy farmer, and gallons of quality milk were poured away, and many good animals sent to premature slaughter.'

'I use the Internet a lot,' Jack said. 'The official ministries and agencies provide authorised information and what is intended to be believed.' Jack said. 'But the unauthorised stuff is more informative. They have reputable sources of knowledge and science that the official sites ignore.'

Mrs Watson cleared their plates away.

'Beth and I often go out for a meal during the week when we are in London,' Jack said, 'but none of them come up to your Sunday roast, Mum.'

Later in the afternoon, Jack helped his father with the afternoon milking.

'It's good to be able to drink the milk from our own cows when I'm home,' Jack said. 'I've had people tell me that they would like to buy unpasteurised milk. It's not illegal to sell it, but increased costs were put on producers making the sales uneconomic. It seems strange, when other foods that are adulterated with manufactured chemicals are sold to the public without any penalty on the producers.'

'When we used to sell our milk to the National Milk Cooperative,' Mr Watson said, 'we knew we had a reliable market and a fair price that enabled us to invest in the farm.' He paused. 'I did hear,' he continued, 'that some of the people who benefitted from the disbandment of the Cooperative had close connections with both politicians and the supermarkets.'

'I've heard that too,' Jack replied.

'So do you think Tom Leach's heifer is going to make any difference?' Mr Watson said.

'Perhaps not on her own, it's a bit much to ask of her, but she is becoming a figurehead for all sorts of campaigns and organisations. People contact us. Beth and I have suggested coalitions – like minded movements working towards a common goal. If it's something that we support, then Honesty can provide added publicity.'

Mr Watson released one group of cows and the next group filed into the parlour to be milked.

'She's raised the profile of working girls like these,' Jack said, attaching the milking machine clusters to the udders of each cow. 'Most people take milk for granted, they buy it in bottles or cartons, but they don't think about the animals that produce it.'

'Nor the farmer,' Mr Watson remarked.

'Honesty has helped people to associate their food with the way it is produced,' Jack continued. 'She's the bovine face of farming – and she's helped people to care about maintaining our own national food production as well as high welfare husbandry.'

'Well, Jack,' his father said, 'I had serious doubts about what you were doing, but it seems Honesty is an idea whose time has come. I take my hat off to you – and to that heifer. These girls here work hard providing the nation with milk, it's about time they had their own representative.'

'Thanks Dad,' Jack said. 'We both appreciate your support.'

~

Honesty had now been an MP for over 12 months and her postbag was still as full as ever. Jack's diary was booked up months in advance with requests to attend meetings and give talks – on top of which he wrote a regular column for a local newspaper.

'Guess where you have been invited to go and give a talk now,' Beth said as Jack came into the office one morning.

'Not too far away, I hope,' he said. 'If I need to stay away over night, I find I'm playing catch up for the next few days.'

'Well I can't see you getting there and back in one day from this venue,' Beth replied.

'Where is it then, the Outer Hebrides? I'd like to speak with the crofters, they're a community I haven't had any dealings with as yet,' Jack said.

'No, just keep going for a few more thousand miles and you'll get there,' she said grinning. 'It's Canada – you've been invited to visit by the Canadian Cattle Association.'

'I've always wanted to visit Canada,' Jack said eagerly, taking the letter. 'Honesty's bloodline originated over there.'

'It's a pity you won't be able to take her with you,' Beth said. 'But it wouldn't be practicable for just a few days what with quarantine and the cost.'

She turned back to the other pile of letters on her desk. 'You certainly get plenty of invitations one way and another since Honesty was elected,' she said. 'There's another letter here inviting you out to lunch.'

'Well if it's only a lunch date it's a lot easier to fit in, and I don't have to prepare a speech. Who's it from?'

'A man named Andrew Carlyle. He doesn't say much more about himself, just says he would like to have discussions with you over lunch. You've got an afternoon free next week. Shall I book it in your diary?'

'Yes please,' Jack replied.

~

Jack also received a lot of requests to visit rural businesses, with or without Honesty. They were such an important part of the rural economy that whenever possible he would visit and listen to what they had to say. He had great sympathy with those who were working hard to build businesses that not only serviced the local community, but also provided employment for local people. He particularly empathised with those involved with the production and sale of food. Jack knew that health and hygiene were all important, but some of the regulations were imposed without an understanding or consideration of specific trades.

'There's just no common sense in all this,' he complained to Mr Drury one evening. 'If only they would consult with the people they are dealing with before issuing all these regulations it would save so much frustration and anger - and money. They do not conduct any research on the causes of a particular problem or whether or not the new impositions are in fact an improvement on what people have been doing for years without ill effect.'

'Bureaucrats owe their existence and their salaries to directives and regulations.' Jim Drury remarked dryly.

'At one time our animals only had to travel a few miles to the abattoir,' Jack said. 'But now we have to take them further. It's not right, not for the animals, nor for the people forced out of business through inappropriate regulations. Slaughter is a necessary part of farming, but that doesn't mean to say we don't want to do the best by our animals. After all we've reared them from birth, nobody wants them to suffer at the end. I get so frustrated,' he continued. 'Honesty was elected to represent our rural community, but I feel we are failing them through no fault of our own.'

'As I have said before, most directives now are out of the hands of our sovereign representatives,' Jim Drury said. 'Career politicians pay lip service to the concerns of their constituents, but they withhold many pertinent facts.'

'Any suggestions as to how we can make a difference?' Jack said. 'I have met and spoken to so many people, but it seems that one man and one heifer are not going to make any impression on such a behemoth.'

'There are and always have been independently minded MPs, who buck the system. They are not appreciated by their parties but the people like them. I know you take your position seriously, but Honesty's presence in the Chamber draws attention to the theatrical qualities of Parliament, Jack. People like mavericks. They like a bit of theatre. A lot of messages can be advanced by means of street theatre. If all the world's a stage, then Honesty is in the spotlight at the moment. She has the appeal of an animal film star. To use an appropriate figure of speech, milk it.'

Jack laughed. 'Yes, I can see what you mean, but don't you think that seeing us as a pair of Disney characters may be counter productive.'

'Believe me, Jack, individuals, or in your case a double act, can make a difference.'

Chapter twelve

Beth had arranged with Mr Carlyle's secretary, that Jack would have lunch with him on the following Wednesday. A particularly expensive hotel had been specified and Jack arrived in good time. He had been invited out on many occasions since Honesty's election, but nothing quite like this. It had appeared that Mr Carlyle had wanted to discuss farming and environmental matters with Jack, but somehow the location he had selected was at odds with what he wished to discuss.

Jack went into the bar. As he looked about, two men approached him.
'Jack, I'm so glad to meet you, I'm Andrew Carlyle,' he held out his hand. 'And this is my friend, Tony Preston.' Jack shook hands with both of them.
Andrew Carlyle put his arm on Jack's shoulder and guided him towards the bar. 'What are you having to drink?'
The three men took their drinks and sat down. 'Tell me, how has Honesty's election affected the perception of farming among the general population?' Mr Carlyle enquired.
'I think more people are taking notice now,' Jack replied. 'She's given farming a face. A lot of people never thought of where their milk and meat came from, but now they link farming with Honesty and her kind. She helps them relate their food with its method of production.'
'And has her election made any impression on the farming community?' Mr Carlyle continued.
'Yes, I think it has,' Jack said. 'She has raised the profile of farmers. She represents their stock and their livelihood. She helps people appreciate that food is produced on a farm

before it appears in the shops and supermarkets.'

'She has certainly been successful in gaining publicity,' Mr Carlyle said. 'Her marketing value must be considerable.'

'I don't think of her in terms of monetary value,' Jack said, feeling the first twinges of suspicion about his companions. He had felt an undefined uneasiness, when the lunch date had been arranged. Mr Carlyle's secretary had given very little information about him or how farming and the environment had related to his business.

'Honesty was elected as an MP to represent her constituents, any publicity she has gained personally is subservient to that,' Jack said.

'Quite right,' Mr Carlyle replied. 'She has the same status as any other MP and we should not fall into the error of regarding her merely as a symbol.'

Jack took a drink from his glass. 'I'm afraid your secretary did not give me very much information about you,' he said. 'Perhaps you could tell me what line of business you are in?'

'Of course, my apologies. I should have explained earlier, but you see the business I am in is involved with so many aspects of farming and food production that to say I represent just one sector would perhaps have given the wrong impression.'

Jack looked straight at him. He recognised that Mr Carlyle was being evasive, while his companion did not speak at all.

'I believe our table is ready,' Mr Carlyle said. 'Let us eat now. There is so much I would like to discuss with you.'

The three men were shown to a table in a quiet part of the restaurant. It appeared that money was no object as Mr Carlyle ordered a bottle of expensive wine and each man chose from the menu. Jack felt uncomfortable. He sensed that these men had an ulterior motive in inviting him to lunch. Usually when he was invited out he could quickly gauge in which direction his host's interests lay, and discussions were frank and open. But with these men he felt a need to be on guard. Throughout the meal, they spoke about the Government and how its policies affected all aspects of the rural economy. The men were friendly and relaxed, but whenever Jack tried to learn more about Mr Carlyle's business, he skilfully avoided specifics, manipulating the conversation, and filling Jack's glass.

After the excellent meal, Mr Carlyle ordered coffee and the three men retired to the lounge. Jack sank into the deep leather chair and, despite his initial misgivings, he was relaxing in the company of these two men.

'Have you thought about what you will do when Honesty retires from Parliament?' Mr Carlyle asked.

'I will go back to my father's farm,' Jack replied.

'That would be a great waste of all the experience you have gained,' Mr Carlyle said.

'I realise that,' Jack said, 'but I never intended to be involved in politics. I feel much more comfortable in a farming environment and in many ways I will be glad to get back to it.'

The men were silent for a moment. 'It is difficult to make a living from farming these days,' Mr Carlyle said. 'Have you thought about enhancing your income by other means?' He lifted his coffee cup and took a drink.

'Of course,' Jack replied. He knew that many farmers had created other business opportunities, while others had made best use of the grants that were available. 'It is naturally advisable to be aware of what options are available.'

Again there was a pause. 'It may be that I could be in a position to help you,' Mr Carlyle said, looking at Jack.

'In what way?' Jack replied.

'My company is involved with food production and methods of farming throughout the world. They employ many people on a consultative basis. You are just the sort of person they are looking for. As I said we are a large company and the remuneration would be appropriate.' Mr Carlyle paused. 'Your experience has a value to us. It could be used to secure the future of your farm and provide investments.'

Ever since Honesty had entered Parliament, Jack had been aware that he was going to have advantages in regard to offers and opportunities that were not available to other people. That was a fact of life associated with status. He had not previously concerned himself with any of the opportunities available, but now that it appeared that he was being offered a position with considerable financial benefits, it seemed that the proposal could well be worth considering.

'I don't know that I have the qualifications that you require of your consultants,' he said.

'You are a practical farmer,' Mr Carlyle said. 'That in itself is a very useful asset. So many people in large businesses these days have no experience of the actual application of the methods they promote.' He paused. 'You also have political connections,' he added.

After his initial suspicions about these men, Jack had enjoyed the conversation and had relaxed, but at the mention of "political connections" he suddenly realised that he had dropped his guard.

'I'm sorry but you still haven't told me the name of your company,' he said.

'As I said we are a large company,' Mr Carlyle smiled. 'You may associate things with a name, which are not appropriate to our present discussion.'

Jack did not return the smile. 'The name of your company?' he repeated.

Mr Carlyle poured himself another cup of coffee, and without looking up he gave the name of a global agrochemical biotech company.

Jack didn't speak. He felt his face flushing. What a fool he had been.

'Jack, do not make any hasty decisions.' He heard Mr Carlyle's voice. 'I can arrange for you to come to one of our corporate week-ends in the country. You can speak to some of our other consultants. You may recognise some of them.'

'No!' Jack looked straight at him. 'There is no way that I would associate with your organisation. You want to use me and my name – and Honesty's name - to endorse a science and a technology that is the very opposite of what I have been promoting since I declared her a candidate for election.'

Mr Carlyle remained calm. 'I know that you do not approve of our technology but you cannot hold back progress. You have very worthy objectives – but are they going to provide you with a secure financial future? Don't make any hasty decisions until you have thought this through, we are talking of the possibility of six figure sums in consultancy fees.'

Jack jumped up. 'I said No! No way!'

He turned and walked out. As he came out of the hotel's main entrance he did not make a decision about his direction of travel. He was angry and upset. Angry and guilty – he had so nearly compromised both himself and Honesty. Of course - there had been the evasion about who they worked for, their ingratiating conversation. He had had his suspicions to begin with, but they had seemed genuinely interested in what he was doing.

He was shocked at how easy it was to be seduced. Wealth was his for the taking – but at what price? Of course, if he had taken up their offer he would, as spokesman for Honesty, have had to declare his interest. But there would naturally be restrictions on his freedom of expression as far as the company's business was concerned, and simply abstaining from adverse comment could be interpreted as support. The corporation would use his name, and that of Honesty, to provide a false façade of integrity to their developments and business dealings. It was corporations like this one which had changed the face of farming around the world, and which had impacted so badly on animal welfare.

His steps slowed down. Now his distress was overcoming his anger. Across the street he saw an entrance to a park. He went into the park. It was a far cry from the fields and woodlands of home, but it would help clear his head. He didn't want to go straight home to Beth. He felt too guilty. She shared his values and he felt that he had been in danger of letting her down.

Jack wanted to visit Honesty – he needed contact with her. She was the connection with the farm back home and what to him were real values. He briskly walked to the nearest tube station and shortly afterwards was letting himself in through the gates of the city farm. All the members of the public had left and the staff had gone home for the night. He made his way to Honesty's loose-box. She was standing nibbling the last few bits of sweet scented dried grass beneath her hay rack. She looked up as he peered over the half door.

'Sorry girl,' he said quietly. 'I so nearly let you down.'

Honesty walked over to him. Although she was used to being the centre of attention, like many animals she could sense the emotions of her human companions. Jack let his one arm hang over the door towards her, and after the briefest of sniffs, she gently caressed the back of his hand with an affectionate lick of her rough tongue.

'Oh Honesty!' he said and dropped his forehead onto his arm. She returned to her hay and Jack stood for a while leaning on the door.

Jack rang Mr Drury later that evening.

'I'm not surprised,' Jim Drury said. 'The only thing that surprises me is the fact it has taken them so long to approach you.'

'So everyone receives the same sort of offers?' Jack said.

'Yes, of course,' Mr Drury replied. 'In fact it is very

often expected now. Corporate lobbyists prowl around the corridors of power in both London and Brussels like predatory animals.' Jack was silent

'People like those who took you out to lunch are always there in the background. They have large expense accounts which they are expected to use to effect. The customary contacts and socialising didn't apply in your case. You are independent – you are not connected to any particular party and you don't belong to the usual clubs.'

'I guess I have always been aware that policies were manipulated away from the public face of opposition and debates,' Jack said. 'It's just that it came as a shock to find how close I was to becoming part of it.'

'Decisions by governments throughout the world are swayed by lobbyists. Inevitably much of that influence is unethical. I'm very glad you kept your honesty and integrity. You have upheld your heifer's name. Her electors may be unaware of the position you found yourself in today, but you have just confirmed their faith in you.'

Following his conversation with Mr Drury, Jack felt better. He told Beth about the meeting.

'I feel torn between wanting to get out of it all, and wanting to stay in order to try and make a difference,' he said.

'I know what you mean,' she said.

'The sort of people I met today are the ones influencing decisions about our lives and our health - all of us human and animal.'

'There are still a lot of people who care about truth and justice,' Beth said. 'Honesty is a beacon for them. She is a focus that encourages them. Your individual stand this afternoon won't change anything, but enough individuals with the same principles, can create a chain reaction.'

Chapter thirteen

'Of course!' Beth looked up, her eyes sparkling with enthusiasm. 'Street theatre, why hadn't we thought of that before.'

Jack had told her about Mr Drury's suggestion several days before. He had thought it quite a good idea at the time, but now Beth appeared ready to get it all up and running as soon as she could. She enjoyed amateur dramatics and had always taken part in any YFC productions.

'I'm afraid they will regard us as Disney characters,' Jack said. 'I have accompanied Honesty to Parliament to speak on her behalf. It is a responsible position and I want to treat it responsibly.'

'Of course you do,' Beth replied. 'I know people admire you for the way you have taken on your responsibilities, but that doesn't mean that we cannot convey your messages by other more playful means.' Jack didn't look convinced.

'You mention Disney,' she continued. 'But don't forget not all of his films were cartoons, there have been other family films which have been very popular with the audiences.'

'Yes,' Jack agreed, 'but I still don't want to involve Honesty in something which would be perceived as superficial and frivolous.'

'Exactly,' Beth responded. 'Provided we research what we want to portray, make sure we have the right players, and produce it in the right place and at the right time, people will watch it and note what we are saying. Don't you remember when we saw some street theatre a few months back at one of the outdoor markets? There was a real vibrancy about the place and people stopped to watch because they enjoyed it.'

'Yes, I remember,' Jack said. 'Well, seeing as you are

so keen, and I've got plenty of work on at the moment, I'll delegate you to arrange something - but I don't want Honesty to have to appear in every production, it wouldn't be fair on her.'

'No I understand that,' Beth said. 'She can make token appearances, but I think a pantomime cow representing her would be much more suitable.'

'A pantomime cow?' Jack looked unhappy.

'Just leave it with me,' Beth said. 'I'm sure I can come up with something you will like.'

After she had sorted out Jack's paperwork and correspondence, Beth started making enquiries about street theatre groups around the capital. Over the next few days both of them went out to visit various performances. Very often they included ethnic minorities, and generally they were very colourful, usually with musical accompaniment. As Beth had said they brought a vibrancy to each location. The audiences were casual, moving around, passing by and sometimes seated on nearby benches or at cafe tables. After watching several performances, Beth approached one group of players. She introduced herself.

'Jack and I would like to join with you in creating some street theatre in which we could explain what Honesty is trying to represent as an MP.'

The group of young men and women looked at each other. A tall Afro Caribbean man spoke first.

'Perhaps we could help you with that,' he said. 'We don't normally do national politics, but we know of Honesty, she's different. Let us know what you want to do and we'll get back to you.'

Back at their office, Beth discussed the project with Jack.

'We ought to present them with the outline of a script,' she said. 'I know they often adapt their words and actions as they go along, so it mustn't be too rigid. What do you think we should use as our first theme?'

'Well it's no use using purely rural issues in an urban situation like this,' Jack said. 'It's got to relate to the people who live around here.'

'Yes,' Beth agreed. 'The obvious subject would be food, the way it is produced, how the price that the shopper pays compares to what the producer gets, but we've got to keep it simple.'

'Then we have to decide where to stage it,' Jack said.

'Somewhere where people eat,' she said.

'Perhaps a fast food outlet,' Jack said.

'Maybe,' Beth replied. 'No, I think an organic café would be best to begin with. I think the customers would be more likely to appreciate the performance, then depending on how it is received we could move on to other locations.'

'The West End, perhaps,' Jack said grinning.

'Why not,' she replied, 'but first I've got to draft out a script.'

After much thought, amendments and alterations, Beth came up with the basis for several short performances. She typed it out and sent it to Nathan, the Afro Caribbean man she had spoken to previously.

About a week later he telephoned her. 'I've discussed your ideas with the rest of the players and we think it could work. If you can come over sometime, we'll give you a short demonstration.'

Beth spoke to Jack and between them they agreed a date. A few days later, they made their way to a community hall in the East End.

'We received a grant to pay for our expenses,' Nathan explained. 'What we do is classed as Arts and Culture. It's good to have somewhere to rehearse and money for costumes, but I feel that now some of our acts lack the spontaneity of our first performances.'

Jack and Beth were introduced to the rest of the performers.

'And this is Lou,' Nathan said, indicating a small wiry man, who grinned at them, as he bobbed about and spun around. 'He is going to be one of our cows. We will show you how we are going to work your ideas then, before we go out on the streets we want to visit Honesty. Perhaps she can give us some tips on how to play at being cows.'

Jack and Beth took their seats and the players moved around the floor, interacting with each other. It was basic theatre.

'It reminds me of Mummers' plays,' Jack whispered to Beth.

'Yes,' she agreed. 'Although this is now played out in an urban setting, they were once performed in the country villages. I think it is so appropriate to involve Honesty's representation of the people in this way. We are bringing the village to the city by means of these players.'

The players visited Honesty at the city farm the following week. Lou joined her in the little paddock, dancing around her, imitating her movements. Honesty, for her part, took little notice of him. To her he was just another human, who performed slightly stranger antics than most.

Beth also made enquiries as to where their little performances could be played out. She made a list of places including the vicinity of some organic establishments. One café was situated within a courtyard and appeared ideal for the first performance. Arrangements were made with the local authority and the players, and a date agreed.

On the appointed day, Jack and Beth travelled to the location. They took Honesty with them in the trailer. They parked near the café, and although Jack didn't take Honesty from the trailer, he lowered the ramp in order that people could see her. He stood beside the trailer talking to people and explaining how he spoke on Honesty's behalf. The weather was warm and sunny, and the streets and shops busy. Nathan and his friends had arrived in a large van, painted in gaudy colours.

Jack and Beth remained by the trailer and watched, while two of the players from the street theatre group started to play musical instruments, moving among the shoppers circulating through the courtyard. Then one by one other players emerged from the back of the van. Lou and three other people were now dressed in a black and white fabric costumes, with horns on their heads and large pink udders in the appropriate places. Each bore a word across their chests: Honesty; Integrity; Truth; Justice. They lined up linking arms swaying to the music.

'Ho there, cows,' one of the other players, dressed as a farmer in breeches and waistcoat and carrying a bucket, approached them. 'I have come to milk you. I need lots of milk because what I am paid is hardly enough to pay my bills.'

'But why are you not paid properly for the milk we give you,' one of the cows responded.

'Because the man from the supermarket says he will not pay more.'

Another player emerged from the van. He carried a clip-board and was dressed in a black suit with an enormous belly with the word "Profit", written across it.

'Mr Farmer I have come to buy your milk,' he said.

'Can you not give the farmer more money to feed us,' the cow labelled Integrity said.

'I cannot,' the man said speaking to the audience and patting his fat belly. 'My customers want cheap food and my shareholders want big dividends.'

'But if the farmer cannot pay his bills he will sell us,' the cow labelled Honesty said, and each of the cows then commenced weeping and wailing.

'That is no concern of mine,' the supermarket man said.

'My cows ask me for herbs to keep them in good health,'

the farmer addressed the audience, 'but I am bound to the supermarket and I cannot afford such luxuries for them.'

The cows raised their voices in more wails. 'Is there no other way,' the cow labelled Truth said, holding her hands together pleadingly.

At that point another player emerged from the van. 'Perhaps I can be of help,' he said. Dressed in a white coat he smiled at the farmer, the cows and the audience.

He addressed the farmer and the cows. 'If your farm becomes organic I will buy your milk and sell it in my shop. My customers like to know where their food comes from. They know I support small producers and that I give a fair price.'

'What must I do to become organic?' the farmer replied.

'Your soil and your crops must be pure – they must not be treated with chemicals.'

'But what about us,' one of the cows said.

'You must have the herbs you need to keep you well,' the man in the white coat said.

'But will you pay a fair price for our milk?' the cow labelled Justice said.

'Of course,' the man replied. 'We will tell our customers that the milk is organic and that it comes from cows named Honesty and Integrity and Truth and Justice.'

The cows smiled at each other. 'Then farmer will not have to sell us,' one cow exclaimed.

'And we can eat the herbs,' another said.

'And I will not longer be bound to the supermarket,' the farmer said raising his stick and chasing the man in the black suit around the courtyard while the cows danced with the man in the white coat, to the accompaniment of the musicians.

At the completion of the little sketch, the performers sat down outside the café and Beth joined them. It appeared to have gone down well with the shoppers, especially the children who had clutched their parents hands and pleaded with them to stay and watch the cows and the farmer.

'We will do another performance again shortly,' Nathan said. 'We have made a selection of sketches from the ideas you gave us and we will tour all the sites you have selected.'

Over the next few weeks, the little street theatre company, performed around many areas of the capital. Beth had given Nathan a list of ideas, including transnational companies and genetic modification, the welfare standards of cheap imports, live exports and global trade. Very often Jack would take Honesty along and speak with local people. Sometimes the local MP for the constituency would join him, realising that to be seen with Honesty would enhance his or her image. Overall, Jack and Beth felt that their venture into theatricals had been a success.

~

Jack and Honesty returned home during the summer recess. Although Jack continued to help out on the farm, he also continued to work hard on Honesty's behalf - answering correspondence, meeting her constituents, and making many visits with her around the country. Beth also helped out, not only with the secretarial work, but accompanying Jack and Honesty to many events. She was a regular visitor at the Watson's farm and sometimes walked across the fields with Jack when he needed a break from the heavy workload.

The cows grazed the pastures between milkings, and both Jack and Beth enjoyed walking among them as the animals lay around in contemplation.

'There's something so serene about cows when they are ruminating, relaxed and contented, in their natural surroundings. It helps me relax too. It's a pity more people can't experience it – it would save the National Health Service a lot of money,' Beth said.

'That's right,' Jack replied. 'I've thought a lot about what Julie said when we visited her farm. Her family had such a rapport with all the animals; they recognised them all as individual characters and the animals responded to them. I don't think any of us realised just how capable they are of understanding and of expressing their feelings. I hope people realise that Honesty is not a one-off, there are millions of others out there with just the same individual personalities.'

They opened the gate and walked onto the farm track.

'Over the past twelve months or so, the more I have seen of some of the other elected representatives in Parliament, I really think that a few more sentient animals at Westminster would raise the standards.'

'Perhaps,' Beth replied. 'But don't forget how Napoleon and the rest of the pigs in Animal Farm turned out.'

'I guess you're right,' Jack said. 'I expect there would always be those who would take advantage.'

~

One week end, Jack and Beth took Honesty to a summer fair at one of the villages in her constituency. Jack, together with Honesty, was to open the proceedings. Many of the prizes were cuddly toy cows. The ladies of the village had baked cakes and biscuits decorated with cows, and the children were invited to "Pin the tail on the Cow".

'We thought of marking out a grid on the field and charging £1 per square. Wherever Honesty did a cowpat whoever had paid for that square would win a prize,' one of the organisers said to Jack. 'But then we thought that it was rather undignified to ask our MP to participate in that manner.'

The fair had also provided the opportunity to get support for a sponsored "Ragwort Pull" and a sponsored "Litter Pick" on behalf of local charities. The day was blessed with good weather and the refreshment tent was doing a good trade. The fair had drawn crowds from quite far afield and a local band, wearing hats trimmed with black and white spotted fabric, played the music.

Jack, Beth and some of their friends from the YFC occupied one end of an open sided tent, while Honesty occupied a pen in the other half.

Children came to see Honesty, and they spoke to her as they did to their pets at home.

Older people came to see Honesty too. The retired farmers among them would lean on the bars of her pen and look at her, as if bidding at auction. Many of them remembered the time, not that long ago, when farming was a major part of village life, when each farm carried a variety of livestock. They enjoyed telling Jack their memories, many of which coincided with what his father and grandfather had told him.

'Never thought I'd see the day a heifer was elected to Parliament,' one elderly man said. 'But then never expected to see farming the way it is today.'

'Too much interference from them as is not connected to the land,' another man said. 'That there heifer got my vote last time. Both her and Jack Watson come from farming stock, they don't hold with all that artificial political talk. Artificial talk is like artificial fertilisers – no real substance to it.'

'Give me honest to goodness cow muck any day,' the first man said. 'That there heifer can produce good cow muck, and Jack Watson can produce honest talk. If that's what we'd have had from our politicians, then we wouldn't be in the mess we're in today.'

Chapter fourteen

Arriving in Canada, Jack was met at the airport by two of his hosts, who drove him to the farm where he would be spending the first few days.

'What are your first impressions of Canada then?' he was asked.

'Everything is on such a big scale, there is so much distance between everything,' he said. 'It makes me realise how small and compact Great Britain is.'

His host ran a large dairy unit and showed Jack around.

Over the next few days, Jack met many other farmers and enjoyed their hospitality. They entertained him in their homes, showed him their farms with pride and enquired about the state of farming in Britain. Which type of farming was the most profitable, what were the main problems and how were farmers responding to them? Were diversification enterprises being successful? What did Jack see as the future for British farming?

'As the spokesman for the British parliament's first, and probably last, bovine MP, I am particularly concerned about the effects of profit driven policies on livestock farmers and their animals,' Jack said. 'The economic assault has struck hardest at small family farms, which were once a vital part of the local economy and local community. They can no longer compete, as their profits are pared away in supermarket price wars, where food is sourced from the cheapest supplier in the world. Cheapest, because they reduce their overheads by ignoring animal welfare. In factory farms, animals - sentient animals - are treated merely as production units.

'There is also the corporate influence on the way farmers operate these days,' Jack continued. He told his host about his meeting with the corporate executives, and confessed to the sense of guilt it had engendered.

'You will never make a politician if you feel guilt,' the farmer responded.

'For some time I have admired the stance of one of your own Canadian farmers, Perkin Schmidt,' Jack said. 'He stood up to one of the biggest corporations against all the odds.'

The farmer agreed, 'He is a courageous man. He stood up for all of us.'

~

After a few days he moved to another area, and was once again treated to Canadian farming hospitality.

'We have read so much about Honesty,' his hostess said. 'We are so pleased you have been able to come and visit us.'

'It really is a privilege to be invited here,' Jack said, 'but I owe my present position entirely to Honesty. I don't think the voters would have elected me if I had stood on my own.'

'It must have been a very strange position you found yourself in when she was elected,' the farmer said.

'Yes, it was at first,' Jack replied, 'but then I realised that Honesty and I were a sort of double act, she provided me with the opportunity to express all the things of concern to the people of her constituency.'

'But as her interpreter are there any restrictions on you?' the farmer's wife enquired.

'Very few,' Jack replied. 'Her election was a unique event, so any problems have to be resolved as we go along. I have an office and a secretary like any other MP, but I must always bear in mind that I must deal with everything with honesty and integrity, because that is why people voted for her. Because I am representing her I also feel obliged to interpret many things from the point of view of a sentient animal. Very often that enables me to approach things from a different angle, and it adds a new dimension to my thinking.'

'We are very much looking forward to the talk you are going to give at the community centre,' the farmer said. 'There has been a great deal of interest; both farmers and townsfolk want to hear what you have to say.'

The following evening, Jack's host and hostess drove him to the community centre in the nearest town. Jack had become used to public speaking by now, but this time there was an international dimension and he welcomed the opportunity to speak on things which had troubled him for some time. At the back of the stage was a large screen which displayed a selection of photographs of Honesty. As his host had stated, there was a great deal of interest and almost all the seats were taken.

The local farmers' representative stood on the stage.

'And now I would like to welcome Mr Jack Watson, the human spokesman for the British MP, Coatewood Integrity Honesty.'

The audience greeted Jack with a round of applause. He looked confident as he took his place behind the podium. His hosts had been very welcoming and he knew that these people appreciated his visit to their country. They had come not only to hear about his experiences as the representative of Britain's first bovine MP, but also to hear his views on matters that affected some of them, as much as they affected Honesty's constituents.

'Good evening, ladies and gentleman,' he began. 'It is a great privilege to be invited here to address you all. However I am very much aware that I owe my position almost entirely to a heifer, albeit a very special heifer. Without her I would not be able to speak on the problems effecting farming and our rural communities, either in Parliament at Westminster or here in Canada. Without her I would have remained the son of an English dairy farmer, helping my father run our farm on a desperately low profit margin. When my friends and I registered Honesty as a candidate at the last British general election, none of us expected her to be elected. But people responded to the probity inherent in her names and sent her to Parliament. It was then incumbent upon me to act in accordance with what her names implied.

'Unfortunately Honesty cannot be here with me today. I would very much like you to have met her. I think she is special, but then I am biased. To almost everyone else she is an ordinary Holstein heifer, and it is in that capacity that she conveys to me what she considers needs to be done to improve the lives of both animals and people on this our shared Earth.'

Jack then spoke about his life at Westminster, how both he and Honesty coped with the situations they encountered, how he dealt with correspondence and personal visits – and how her election had affected both their lives.

The meeting he had had with the two corporate executives, who had tried to entice him to abandon his principles with promises of wealth and position, was still fresh in his memory, and drove his thoughts and words.

'However one of my main concerns at this present time is in regard to multinational corporations, and efforts to dominate not only trade, but also the life and soul of nations. They are compromising not only the integrity of animal husbandry, but also the very fabric of the soil, on which life on earth depends.'

The audience clapped.

He thought of what he had read, about farmers in developing countries driven to suicide by the failure of their crops, following applications of the new science. Science developed, not with humanitarian motives, but as a means of cornering the market for seeds and herbicides, until there was no longer any competition. Some water supplies in these same nations had failed, when aquifers had been drained as a result of unsustainable corporate activity. The local populations had been regarded as dispensable.

'The tentacles of these corporations reach into every corner of the world. They have no conception of honourable behaviour. They are motivated entirely by power and greed. Whole populations are effected by their drive to dominate all aspects of food production, by chemical, scientific and technical as well as economic means. There are no countries on earth that are not affected to a greater or lesser degree. I know that all of you are aware of the contamination of non GM crops by neighbouring GM crops in this country, and the subsequent litigation brought by the corporation against the innocent party.' Jack paused. He could sense that the audience were on his side as he delivered his last point.

He continued.

'These corporations continue with further scientific research in order to create more power and more profits. Research that would see the destruction of farming as we know it - and the enslavement of generations of producers, not only in the Third World but eventually in your country and mine.'

Jack took a sip from his glass at his side. 'Other scientific research which goes against these technologies is being suppressed. Scientists are not being allowed to voice their concerns or publish their findings. Unaccountable forces, seemingly beyond our control, are preventing us from knowing the truth. Reports of animals suffering and adverse effects from genetic manipulation are being concealed. This is not only of concern to me for it's effect on the animals, but also the possibility, that in the future those effects are going to be experienced by the human population. Even as I speak scientists and technicians are forging ahead with ever more potent manipulations, which will affect all life on earth.

'As the spokesperson for Coatewood Integrity Honesty MP, I ask that you all remember the native people of this continent and how they lived in harmony with the land and their fellow creatures. As the present day custodians we need to assert independence from the corporations, embrace sustainability and reawaken our respect for all our fellows be they human or animal. On behalf of Honesty I would like to thank you all for inviting me here to speak tonight. You have given me a most warm welcome to your country, and I am very sorry that Honesty could not have been here with me as I know she would have received an equally generous welcome both from yourselves and from the many Canadian cattle I have met over the past week. Thank you.'

The audience clapped enthusiastically. The farmers' leader returned to the stage.
'I'm sure Mr Watson has given us a lot to think about this evening,' he said. 'Are their any questions?'
Several members of the audience asked questions, after which the farmer's leader concluded, 'Thank you Jack. We understand and accept that your position is as Honesty's interpreter, however we think that she is singularly fortunate in having you as her spokesman. If those are Honesty's own views that you have expressed this evening then I think it is about time that we had some cows and heifers elected to our own Canadian Parliament.'
Many of the people joined Jack in the hospitality suite afterwards. The farmer with whom he was staying came up to him.
'You certainly spoke your opinions,' he said. 'And it was very much appreciated by the audience. I hope you will be able to visit us again.'

The following day Jack was driven to the airport. He thanked his host.
'It has been our pleasure,' the farmer said. 'And give

our kind regards to Honesty. I will be looking at my cows in a new light now. I will be wondering what deep thoughts they are concealing under those placid expressions.'

Chapter fifteen

Neither Jack nor Beth liked living in London, both of them were anxious to return to the country. Honesty herself showed little preference either way. She liked her quarters at the city farm, and took her visits to Parliament as part of her routine. If she ever wondered why there were no other cattle or other animals within the Palace of Westminster, she never showed it.

Jack always looked forward to returning home as often as possible. He felt it helped to "ground" him after the alien atmosphere of the Westminster parliament. After working on the land and taking responsibility for the lives and welfare of farm animals, the posturing and pettiness he encountered there irritated him.

'Did you tell them that two more farmers round here have given up in the past few months?, Mr Watson asked his son. 'They've sold their stock - they can't make a living from it anymore.'

'I know Dad,' Jack replied. 'I write to the ministers, but they are detached from the effects of their policies – there's no connection with what people are experiencing.'

~

Over the past eighteen months, most of the other MPs had come to regard him and Honesty with indifference, but he felt a distinct hostility from some others. Some women members were more friendly; it was as if they were supportive of another female, albeit a bovine one.

'I would invite Honesty to the lady members' room,' one woman MP said to Jack. 'But I'm afraid you would not be admitted, and I'm not sure that any of the other lady members would be prepared to act as her escort.' She scratched the side of Honesty's neck, but was careful to keep her clothing out of reach of Honesty's questing tongue. Other women ignored Honesty, particularly those who had supported measures that had impacted badly on the lives of farm animals and poultry.

Jack had only once spoken with the Prime Minister, but came away from the encounter feeling that the Prime Minister had merely spoken empty words with an equally empty smile. He knew that many MPs resented Honesty's pen occupying space in the Chamber, where seating was often at a premium - and on the occasions when Jack spoke in the Chamber on her behalf, he sensed their antagonism. This became more pronounced if Jack spoke against any measures which they supported.

~

During the following week, a debate took place regarding proposed regulations concerning the development of farm shops. Jack, on Honesty's behalf, spoke passionately on the need to reduce the red tape which was hindering and constricting both established farm enterprises, and also putting off prospective entrepreneurs. Since Honesty was elected he had received a considerable amount of correspondence on this very topic. The ministerial spokesman argued on the other hand, that such regulations were necessary to safeguard consumers by way of constant inspections, which the shop keeper must pay for, as well as the necessity of regular written records which must be forwarded to the appropriate agency before being returned with the required stamp of approval.

'These regulations will suffocate initiative and enterprise,' Jack cried. 'The people who create and run these shops usually have high animal welfare standards, which they are proud to convey to their customers. This is something that Honesty strongly supports. Very often these farmers rear rare breeds of livestock, and this should be encouraged to provide genetic variation, which often incorporates disease resistance.' Jack looked around the Chamber. Some members nodded approval of what he was saying, but it seemed that others showed little interest, and Jack felt that supporting their party was more important to them than making personal commitments in line with the best interests of their constituents. Some of these were the men who were opposed to Honesty's membership of the House, and showed their disregard whenever Jack spoke on her behalf.

'We need to encourage people to develop enterprises which will serve the community and create viable farm businesses,' he continued. 'The well-being of the local economy is dependant upon them.'

The ministerial spokesman appeared unimpressed. 'We are assured by health officials and agency scientists that these regulations are necessary,' he replied.

Jack sighed and sat down.

At this point one of the other MPs stood up.

'Mr Speaker,' he said grinning towards Jack and Honesty. 'The Honourable Member for Leythorpe Valley naturally has an interest in the promotion of farm shops - as she is quite likely to end up in one as stewing steak and beefburgers.'

Jack leapt to his feet, along with some other MPs, as the Chamber erupted in laughter and shouts of 'Shame!'

'Order! order!' shouted the Speaker. 'The Honourable Member will withdraw that remark immediately.'

The MP stood up 'Indeed Mr Speaker, I withdraw my remarks that the Honourable Member may be turned into beefburgers.' He sat down again, smirking, amid some heckling and subdued laughter.

'Order, order,' the Speaker said again as some degree of decorum returned to the Chamber. Jack looked at the MP with contempt. He looked at Honesty quietly chewing her cud and thought that even as a four-legged animal she stood head and shoulders above many of the people present, in her gentle humility. When he was required to speak for her, Jack felt it essential that he should draw on the qualities of Honesty and her kind, and speak with dignity and truthfulness, and state the views of her constituents who had entrusted her with their representation.

As Jack and Honesty left the Commons Chamber and headed towards the rear entrance where the trailer was parked, several of the men, who Jack recognised as the ones who disliked her, jostled around her. They seemed unnecessarily close, and as Jack held the halter rope her could feel her becoming agitated by the proximity of these people.

'Moo,' one of the men said pushing against her. Honesty now started to twist around. 'Leave her alone,' Jack said angrily.

'Why don't you take her back to the farm where she belongs,' another said as they continued to crush around her. Jack felt sure they were poking and prodding her. 'Leave her alone,' he repeated. 'She has as much right to be here as you.'

'Moo, moo,' they said, as Honesty continued to turn about.

'Aagh!' one of the men suddenly cried, 'She's stood on my foot.'

'Serves you right,' Jack shouted as he pulled Honesty away. The men moved off along the hallway, speaking unnecessarily loudly with occasional guffaws, while their companion limped along behind them.

'Good on you, girl,' Jack said to Honesty as he stroked her neck. 'Pity you didn't tread on a few more feet.'

'I'm sorry about that, Jack.' Jack turned to see one of the women members standing close by. 'The conduct of some of those men is disgraceful, their behaviour reflects badly on the rest of us.' She scratched Honesty's nose.

'I had been warned about some of the tactics that are used here, but it still shocks me that people in respected positions in society can act in this way,' Jack replied.

'Yes, sadly it is something that they have grown up with,' the woman said. 'You have to remember that many of these men experienced this sort of behaviour at school, and carried it on into their adult life. It is very much a case of them knowing no better.'

Another woman joined them.

'Hello there, Honesty,' she said, giving her a stroke. 'I hope you didn't take those offensive comments to heart.'

All three people looked at Honesty, who had calmed down and stood patiently waiting for Jack to lead her out to her trailer.

'No, she just treats those sort of remarks with disdain,' Jack replied.

'Would you like to come and have tea with us,' one of the women enquired.

'That's very kind of you,' Jack said. 'But I need to get Honesty back to the city farm and get her settled down for the evening.'

'It's a great pity that she can't join us in the tea rooms as well, we girls need to stick up for one another,' the woman said.

'Thanks,' Jack said. 'She appreciates your moral support.'

Later that evening Jack rang Mr Drury and told him about the afternoon's events.

'Yes, sounds familiar,' he said. 'You will find that however much you may explain the benefits of less regulation or the social and economic good sense of a particular business, technology or activity, you will be opposed by the status quo. As I have explained before, much legislation and regulation originates outside this parliament and the Government has no option but to approve it. Added to which the regulatory bodies have their own empires to promote and sustain.'

Jack sighed. 'I'm trying my best, but it seems like real progress towards a more just society is not really on the agenda.'

'Don't be discouraged.' Mr Drury said. 'The fact that you are there, representing Honesty, and speaking sincerely on things you believe in, is an antidote to much of the pointless rhetoric that often passes for debate. People appreciate you for it.'

'I know people appreciate what I am doing,' Jack said. 'But I also feel that I am being unfair to Honesty in exposing her to the spiteful behaviour that she experienced this afternoon.'

'I'm afraid that is sometimes the case, the ladies you mentioned were right in their explanation for the bullying tactics. Some of those men still resent women in the House. The fact that Honesty is not only a different species but is also female means they despise her on two counts. Strange as it may seem, she may not have encountered such hostility if she had been a bull.'

Chapter sixteen

The night was dark, and a new moon appeared now and then among the clouds, as four figures made their way along the paths and around the buildings.

'Here it is,' a man's whispered voice broke the silence, as he stood outside Honesty's loose box at the city farm. He knew the location from his previous visits. As such a well-known resident of the farm, the location of her quarters were easily found. The door of the loose box was bolted but not locked, and the four darkly clad people went inside.

Honesty had been ruminating to herself, and was not unduly surprised by the unexpected visitors. She had become so used to being taken to the most unusual places both day and night over the past 18 months, that she took such a nocturnal visit in her stride. She stood up - but there was something about these people that made her uneasy. Usually it was Jack and Beth who came to fetch her, and she had become used to the staff at the city farm who attended to her needs, but she did not know these people and she backed away from them.

'Come along, Honesty,' a woman's voice said, but it was not Beth, and Honesty was not reassured. Although she was suspicious of them she did not try to prevent them attaching a rope to her halter, and she followed as they led her from the loose box.

The four people, now with Honesty in tow, retraced their steps through the farm - an occasional shuffling movement in the straw the only indication of the presence of the other inhabitants. The three men and one woman led her round the back of the farm where visitors did not normally go and through some gates, where a box wagon was parked. They lowered a ramp and led Honesty inside. A few minutes later the engine started and the wagon was driven off down the road.

~

Jack and Beth had just arrived at their office. Jack was not intending to attend the House today and was hoping to catch up on some correspondence.

The phone rang.

'Hello.' Beth recognised the voice of the city farm manager.

'Did you fetch Honesty early this morning?' he said.

'No,' Beth said surprised. 'Why do you ask?'

'When one of the girls went to give her her breakfast, she was not there and the loose-box door was open. We've checked all round the farm and there is no trace of her.' Beth felt a slight shiver as she realised the implication of what he was saying.

'Are there any indications of what has happened?' she said, waving her arm at Jack to attract his attention.

'Well we have discovered the chain securing the rear gates has been cut by a bolt cutter,' the farm manager replied.

'Oh no!' Beth said, looking shocked. 'Have you told the police?'

'Not yet, I needed to check with you first - that you hadn't taken her.'

'We'll be right over,' Beth said, putting the phone down.

The police were already there when Jack and Beth arrived and were taking statements from the staff.

'It seems that Honesty was taken in the middle of the night. Tyre marks indicate that a wagon was parked near the rear gates,' a police inspector informed them.

'Have you passed this information out,' Jack enquired.

'That's where we have a problem,' the inspector replied. 'Normally we would deal with the theft of a farm animal by circulating the details within our own area and making enquiries at likely places of disposal, but as Honesty is an MP, and a high profile MP at that, we are going to have to treat it as kidnapping.'

'So how will you proceed?' Jack said.

'Usually in cases of kidnapping we prefer that the media does not broadcast what has happened, in case it jeopardises the safe return of the victim. Have you received any communication from the kidnappers?' he enquired.

'No nothing yet,' Beth replied.

'I would imagine that you will receive something within the next 24 hours,' the inspector said.

Jack and Beth returned to their office at Westminster, shocked and unhappy.

'I do hope they treat her kindly,' Beth said.

Jack was silent. He had grown very fond of Honesty. He had learned her ways of expressing herself, her little foibles and her way of responding to other people. Like Beth, he could not bear that she be treated harshly.

'I feel so helpless.' he said.

~

No phone calls from the kidnappers were received either by Jack and Beth, the city farm or the police throughout that day. The following morning Beth scanned quickly through the mail, and discovered a letter which drew her attention. She quickly opened it.

'We have Honesty,' the typed letter stated. *'She is quite safe and will remain so while in our care. We are very*

concerned about the proposed development in the countryside adjacent to the proposed new motorway. We care deeply for all its natural beauty - the plants and the trees and the wild inhabitants of the valley, as well as the lake, which is to be filled with industrial waste. Despite the objections of the local inhabitants and serious environmental concerns, the development is to go ahead. We believe that Honesty would support us in this matter. She will remain in our care until we are given reassurances that our concerns and objections are properly addressed.'

'Thank goodness they are taking good care of her,' Beth said.

'Yes, but we still need to get her back as soon as possible,' Jack replied.

'What do you know of this development they refer to?' Beth asked.

'I know of it,' Jack said. 'Although there were independent investigations which showed that the development was flawed - and a lot of local opposition, the findings of an Enquiry went against them. At the time it was felt that the developers had somehow influenced the outcome of the Enquiry. There was a lot of suspicion but not much fact.'

'So these people have felt the need to resort to kidnapping to get to the truth of the matter; it doesn't say much for fairness and justice in the enquiry process does it?'

'I can sympathise with their frustration, but not their method of dealing with it,' Jack replied.

~

The police inspector held the letter, now enclosed in a plastic cover.

'Apart from the postmark it gives us no clues.' he said. 'But as these people promise Honesty's well-being and there are no demands for cash payment, I think we can let the media loose on this.'

Jack and Beth were relieved. They both felt that public knowledge would help facilitate Honesty's return.

'HONESTY KIDNAPPED!' the headlines screamed. **'Where is our Bovine MP?'**

The papers relished the story, even more so than her election, as her popularity was now that much greater. Several pages were devoted to what had happened - with photographs and diagrams of the city farm and the route the kidnappers had taken. Speculation on Honesty's whereabouts was rife, with pages of newsprint devoted to imaginative stories. The papers also covered the reasons for her kidnap with in depth studies into the proposed development, and the objections raised but overruled at the enquiry.

~

In the first few days following the announcement of the kidnap, public opinion was against the kidnappers. People saw Honesty as not just representing farming and rural matters, but championing all their concerns with regard to truth and justice - and her popularity was immense. But as the days passed and they learned more of the reason behind the kidnap, people began to sympathise with the kidnappers motivation, and slowly public opinion began to increasingly place the blame on the politicians and the system that they were a part of.

Initially, the government had no intention of giving way, or even negotiating with the kidnappers. But they were aware that the longer they held out against the demand for a full and fair enquiry into the proposed development, the more people would suspect that there was something to hide. Also, it was quite likely that other issues which they wished to remain obscured and undisclosed would surface and become the object of media scrutiny. Already there were reports of other individuals contacting the press with similar complaints to those of the kidnappers.

Senior members of the government fumed inwardly. Because they courted public support they found that they must of necessity show deep concern for the wellbeing of the heifer, even though many of them resented her popularity.

MPs who suspected that they might lose their seats at the next general election due to what was presently taking place, were particularly hostile to Jack at this time and one MP was overheard to remark, 'If he had not paraded through the streets with that confounded animal in the first place, none of this would have happened.'

As the days passed, Jack found his position was uncertain. With Honesty still missing and her whereabouts unknown - and even the possibility that she was no longer alive - he could hardly be considered to be speaking on her behalf, although he continued with constituency work as her representative. He was very concerned about Honesty, despite the kidnappers reassurances - he could not be sure that they knew the correct food to give her and, in the event of her becoming ill they were unlikely to call a vet.

While the politicians dithered, Jack requested and was given leave to speak in the Chamber. He stood up.

'Throughout the months that I have acted as Honesty's spokesman,' Jack said, ' I have met people - including many farmers - corresponded with many more, raised issues and spoken in debates all with a view to bringing justice and fairness into local and national governance. People are constantly contacting me with cases of burdensome regulation and judgments by which they are having to abide, all without scrutiny of the full facts and no consideration as to how it impacts upon their lives and their businesses. I speak now not only on behalf of Honesty and her constituents – but also for all the people who feel disempowered by a system in which decisions are taken without due regard for local democracy.'

He looked at the straw bedded pen beside him - now empty and forlorn.

'You have failed us.' Jack cried directing his words to both sides of the Chamber. 'These people took Honesty because they had lost faith in the system, and in justice.'

Government Ministers sat stony faced, while some back benchers glared at him and shifted uncomfortably, and a few glanced towards him in covert concurrence. The opposition enjoyed the discomfort of the government, whose minister had been involved with the disputed planning decision, but as Jack's condemnation had been addressed equally to them they felt unable to confront the government as they would have liked.

The longer the matter was taking to be resolved, the more people were remembering instances that had occurred many years before, which both the present government and opposition had considered safely buried. The public had been exhorted to "Move on", assured that lessons had been learned, but now it seemed that the past, like Marley's ghost, was returning to haunt them.

There were now indications that individuals and organisations, who had experienced the maladministration of various government agencies and departments, were joining forces to call for open and truthful investigations. The government were desperate to keep the lid on the smouldering anger, which the issues behind Honesty's kidnap had ignited. If it continued for much longer, who knew what else might be revealed. Where people had once felt that they were powerless in the face of overweening authority – they were now beginning to realise that they could bring about change.

Questions were also starting to be asked openly, and increasingly loudly, about the extraordinary power and authority of the unelected commission under whose influence the Westminster parliament now appeared to operate – passing the laws and regulating the lives of all its citizens. People demanded to know why they had not been told the truth, and why British sovereignty had apparently been given away.

As one foreign correspondent noted dryly, 'It is not beyond the bounds of possibility that both the British government and opposition could be brought down by a cow named Honesty.'

Meanwhile, powerful interests watched silently from the shadows - and in a secluded barn many miles away, a white Holstein heifer lay chewing her cud, serenely contemplating her world with docile equanimity.

Throughout the following days, Ministers and senior politicians walked the corridors of Westminster and Whitehall with anxious faces. They certainly cared little for the welfare of the heifer, but they were acutely aware of the unwelcome spotlight that the kidnap had thrown onto the workings of power and influence. Cabinet meetings were hurriedly arranged.

Just as it seemed that the growing resentment of years of injustice and deception was likely to come to a head, the media suddenly lost interest in the story - and where it had once made front page news, now there were just occasional small items on the inside pages - and instead, pages of newsprint and air time were devoted to a recent sex scandal involving two well known celebrities.

~

As more days passed with no further word from the kidnappers, Jack and Beth were becoming increasingly concerned. Throughout the working day, Beth and the other staff sorted through the large amount of mail that the kidnap had generated. She had not involved herself with the growing furore now engulfing the government, but was desperately anxious for Honesty's safe return. She threw herself into the work, but in the evenings she became tearful, despite the assurances in the kidnappers' letter.

'There is no way we can contact them,' she said. 'Our hands are tied - there is nothing we can do to bring this business to an end and get Honesty returned.'

'We've just got to hope that they will get in touch again,' Jack said. Although he showed less emotion, he missed the presence of the young heifer. 'But until they get what they regard as a satisfactory outcome to the development proposal, they may not see any need to contact us.'

'I'm going to ask the newspapers to ask the kidnappers to get in touch with us.' Beth said. 'Or at least let us know that Honesty is OK.'

Despite their sudden lack of interest recently, the newspapers were only too willing to help out and published Beth's plea. Consequently a few days later another letter was received at the office.

'*Honesty is well,*' it said. '*She has become a great favourite with us, but we will return her, when we are reassured that the countryside is saved.*'

'It seems there is not much more we can do,' Beth said.

'I'll have another word with the Minister.' Jack said. 'The people want Honesty returned to Parliament, and public pressure on the government regarding the disputed development is growing. I don't think they can hold out much longer. If the press print this latest communication from the kidnappers it may make the difference. I don't think it will be long before we see her again.'

~

The newspapers duly printed the kidnappers' latest communication in response to Beth's plea, and a few days later the minister in charge of planning permission summoned both Jack and the MP for the proposed development site to his office.

'I have decided that a further enquiry is in order regarding this particular development.' he said. 'Omissions and discrepancies in the previous hearing make it necessary to hear all the evidence again.'

He looked at Jack and the other man. 'I do not like the way in which this has come about, but if justice is seen to be done, then Honesty will be restored.'

He smiled at his own wit, and Jack smiled at the anticipated happy conclusion to the unhappy circumstances.

As the news of the new enquiry circulated, Jack and Beth waited expectantly for further communication from the kidnappers.

Early in the morning, a couple of days later, one of the newspapers received a phone call stating that Honesty had been placed in a field some miles from the proposed development. The newspaper made sure its reporter and cameraman were well on their way before they rang the police and notified Jack.

Jack and Beth immediately collected the Land Rover and trailer and set off to the given location. When they arrived, journalists, police and a rather bemused looking farmer were already there - and standing by the gate, was the welcome sight of Honesty, ears pricked forward, peering about her as if enjoying the latest bout of attention.

Beth and Jack ran from their vehicle. Beth put her arms round Honesty's neck, sobbing with relief and delight. The newspaper cameraman took photographs, certain of a scoop, while the reporter was busy recording comments from the police and the farmer, whose field had randomly been chosen by the kidnappers as the location for her release.

'Well, Jack,' the reporter said, 'what does it feel like to get her back.'

'It feels great,' Jack said beaming. 'We've missed her so much. People have been so kind and we've had a huge postbag of letters of support. We knew she was popular but the response amazed us. We cannot have asked for greater support. We will now be taking her back to Westminster to continue the job she was elected to do.'

Chapter seventeen

Honesty's arrival back at Westminster was met in the main with good wishes and benevolence. The first time she took her "seat" in her pen, following the kidnap, many members applauded. Those back benchers who were supportive of Jack welcomed her return, while senior members of both parties were exceedingly relieved that the situation which had been developing, had been diffused.

Following her kidnap Jack had been thinking seriously about her future. The present Government still had two or three years to run before another general election, by which time she would be four or five years old. Tom Leach had telephoned Jack. He had no other heifers of Honesty's bloodline and he was anxious that she should bear a calf, preferably before she got much older. Honesty herself had been remarkably adaptable to all the travelling about. It seemed that most of the time she relished the attention. But Jack increasingly appreciated that the continued travelling and her appearances in Parliament were not a normal situation for a dairy heifer. If she did become pregnant, as Mr Leach desired, she could at least take maternity leave.

~

Jack sat in the office with Beth. She passed some letters to him and he opened them. 'Well, well,' he said. 'It looks as if the Prime Minister has discovered a way to remove Honesty from the Commons.'
 'How's that?' Beth replied.
 'He has recommended her for a peerage – he wants to send her to the House of Lords!'

Beth took the letter from Jack. 'Baroness Honesty,' she said. 'It sounds good to me. Do you think I will have to curtsey to her?' Beth grinned.

Jack leaned back in his chair and mulled over the possibilities.

'She has been recommended for Services to Farming and the Environment,' Beth read.

'Basically, they want to pension her off,' Jack said. 'Ever since she entered Parliament I think they have been looking forward to her resignation or retirement. The Government in particular have little empathy with animals, particularly farm animals. The Prime Minister does not like Honesty, I'm sure of that. Her presence and her popularity are a continual irritation to him. I think he will be very relieved if she accepts the title.'

'Will you accept the peerage for her?' Beth asked.

'I'll have to think about it,' Jack replied. 'I cannot see that it would be a practical proposition for her to take her seat in the Lords in the same way that she has a pen in the Commons, and anyway Tom Leach has been saying that he wants a calf from her sooner rather than later. Last time I went home he asked me when he can arrange to get her inseminated.'

'Do you think Tom would give her special treatment when she joins his herd?' Beth asked.

'He has assured me that he will retire her when she has had one or two calves.' Jack said. 'I'm hoping that she can then come and live with us.'

~

Jack and Beth visited the city farm that evening. Security was much tighter now. They went to Honesty's loose-box. She was comfortably bedded, nibbling at the fresh straw.

'Well young lady, how do you feel about becoming

a baroness?' Jack said. Honesty came over to him and he scratched the top of her head.

'Honesty has achieved a lot in the past 18 months, a lot more than many other MPs. She deserves her elevation to the peerage.'

'What about her constituents?' Beth asked.

'There would have to be a by-election of course.' Jack said. 'It would also mean that I could no longer be her spokesman. It would be the end of our campaigning and all the things we've championed together.'

'Not necessarily,' Beth replied. 'Not if you stood as a candidate in your own right.'

'But would people vote for me without my beautiful bovine companion?' he said.

'They voted for her because of her names.' Beth said. 'That is your answer.'

~

Over the next few days, Jack thought about Honesty's future. The kidnap had been a turning point - he did not want to expose her to any more unwarranted stress and the recommendation of a peerage appeared to be an ideal answer. What she had achieved in bringing so many issues regarding farming and rural life to the attention of the general public would be recognised and rewarded. She would not return to the herd simply as another heifer – she would have a status within the cattle community and her title would elevate her even above those high ranked Holsteins, whose names were recognised and respected by farmers throughout the world.

To Jack it seemed that a peerage would suit Tom Leach, as well as the Prime Minister – and remove Honesty from the unnatural environment in which her election had placed her. He asked Beth to send a letter of acceptance.

'I shall have to get used to calling her Lady Honesty,' she said.

The announcement of her peerage would appear in the New Years Honours list but before that, the question of her title had to be agreed. Jack decided that she should be known as Baroness Honesty of Coatewood Farm. A few days later the artificial inseminator visited Honesty at the city farm.

Along with the documents relating to her peerage, Jack was informed that Honesty was entitled to wear the parliamentary robes of a baroness. At first it seemed unnecessary to apply for them, but Beth remarked that Honesty should at least have a robe to indicate her rank.

Jack contacted the tailors who made up the robes and they, after initial misgivings, agreed to make up a rug of scarlet wool cloth which could be laid across her back. Jack insisted that the white trimmings should be made of artificial fur.

~

Some weeks later, the vet confirmed that Honesty was pregnant. Jack rang Tom Leach to inform him, but like prospective parents, Jack and Beth kept her condition secret for the time being.

Before her peerage and her pregnancy became public, Jack continued with his duties as Honesty's spokesman. He still felt passionately about all the issues he had become involved in as a result of her election. He wanted to continue to support them and serve her constituents as long as possible.

'I can't believe it is less than two years since that evening she was elected,' he said. 'So much has happened, we've met so many people and had so much support.'

He rang Jim Drury to inform him of the forthcoming events.

'Congratulations on both counts,' he laughed. 'I must admit the Prime Minister has played a clever hand in sending her to the Lords. I expect it will be a popular decision with the public - and get her, and what she stands for, out of his hair. How do you feel about it all?'

'I'm glad she is receiving recognition for what she has done, even though I realise that her elevation to the Lords is simply a means of removing her from the Commons.'

'She will certainly be a hard act to follow, but whoever gets elected in her place must continue to uphold the values inherent in her names,' Mr Drury said. 'Will you stand yourself?'

'I've thought about that,' Jack said. 'But strange as it may sound I would miss her very much if I was elected in my own right. I was always there for her, but she was also there for me. I will join her when she returns to the farm - neither of us are really cut out for city life. I miss the countryside. I am very grateful that I have been able to speak for Honesty – and with all the publicity I think we have achieved quite a bit. Tom Leach's heifer has enabled me to raise awareness of a lot of things. Now someone else must carry the baton forward.'

~

On the announcement of her pregnancy, Honesty once again made news and Jack and Beth received many letters, cards and emails of congratulations. Journalists and reporters asked Jack about his intentions, and about his impressions of the Westminster Parliament. He explained his decision to return to practical farming.

'I found Parliament so very divorced from the realities of small scale rural economies,' he said. 'Everything is geared to globalisation, which is destroying communities not only here, but also in the developing world. Increasing numbers of people are recognising the need for small scale sustainability, but this is not being supported by government decision makers.'

'Do you think Honesty's election will have any lasting effects?' a journalist asked.

'I think Honesty has brought livestock rearing and welfare to people's attention. Farm animals are no longer seen as production units – they have faces, and their well-being must be factored in to the price paid for milk, meat and eggs. The contract between the producer, the retailer and the consumer must involve fair prices and high welfare standards – and control of animal disease must use available technology and vaccines and must not rely on cruel and outdated methods of eradication.'

'What do you think Honesty's legacy will be?' another asked.

'I have been told that she has created a climate in which changes can eventually take place,' Jack said. 'Personally, I want to see justice and fairness in everything take place immediately. Justice and fairness are not things that should be debated and negotiated over months and even years - they are an inalienable right of all people - and as we are talking here about my speaking on behalf of a heifer - they extend to justice and fairness in all our dealings with the animal kingdom as well. We can learn a lot from the animals, they are not hypocritical - they do not dissemble.' He thought back to Honesty's kidnap. 'We the people need faith in honest representation, and in truth and justice in administration, if not, then the whole system is compromised.'

'Honesty has been a catalyst,' he continued. 'She has enabled people to realise that change is possible. The electorate should apply critical thought to everything they are told both by official spokespersons and in the mainstream media. The voters of Leythorpe Valley did not vote for the regular parties because they did not want more of the same. They recognised what they were looking for in a heifer with the names Honesty and Integrity.'

~

At the Christmas Parliamentary recess, Honesty returned to the farm of her birth. It had been decided that she would not return to Westminster, but would be registered as taking maternity leave.

Mr and Mrs Leach had been somewhat taken aback at the news that their heifer was to have the title of Baroness.

'Well it's no use her putting on any airs and graces when she's with the other cows,' Tom Leach said. 'She'll not get any special treatment from them.'

'I don't think you'll have to worry about her taking advantage of her rank,' Jack said, grinning. 'She's a very egalitarian heifer.'

'What about her calves,' Mrs Leach said, a look of puzzlement on her face. 'Are they going to have titles too.'

'No,' Jack replied. 'It's a Life Peerage – only for her lifetime.'

The Leachs' had had little involvement with all the media attention when Honesty had been staying at the Watson's farm, but on the formal announcement of her peerage in the New Years Honours list, they found their farm the focus of attention on New Year's morning. Jack and Beth had anticipated what would happen and arrived early to prepare for interviews and photo calls.

As the first cameramen arrived, Jack went to fetch Honesty. Beth had already spent some time grooming her, and now the two of them escorted her across the farmyard to the waiting newsmen. As they turned the corner, the cameras clicked and video operators trained their lens on her, as resplendent in her scarlet Parliamentary robe, Baroness Honesty of Coatewood Farm looked about her, eyes bright and black tipped ears forward, she graciously accepted the attention on the culmination of her public life.